THE PENTAGONAL COVEN
A PARANORMAL SAPPHIC WHY CHOOSE ROMANCE

MADISON NICOLE

MN BOOKS LLC

Cover: Amanda Hawkins at Eternal Geekery

Editing & Proofreading: Alexa Thomas at Fiction Fix

❀ Created with Vellum

For my horny besties who just want to be absolutely
railed by several femmes at once.
Let those unhinged thoughts be free.

Before you read...

This book is intended for mature audiences (18+) and reader discretion is advised. This is a kinky why choose erotica. Please keep that in mind while reading. There is a happily ever after but heavy on the spice and less on the plot. If you're like, sign me up! Here is what to look out for:
- Kidnapping
- Threats of sexual assault
- Threats of physical violence
- Murder (not one of the main characters)
- Gore and blood

-Sexual Content: masturbation, hair pulling, branding, biting, anal penetration, choking, vaginal penetration, oral, fingering, collaring, sadism, masochism, voyeurism, temperature play, power dynamics, blood play, toys (dildos, plugs, vibrators), edging, group sex, spanking, orgasm denial, praise, restraints, blindfolds, etc.

If you have any concerns about the contents of this book feel free to email the author, Madison Nicole, at info@madisonnicolebooks.com. Your mental health matters.

ONE

"Don't make a sound," a husky voice whispered in my ear. It was unfamiliar but sounded female. My heart threatened to beat out of my chest as sweat rolled down my forehead.

I swallowed and tried not to jump out of my skin. This was not good. Nothing had gone as planned, and here I was, captured like an absolutely dumbass. Anger rolled through my body, hot and prickly underneath my skin. I was always careful, and I foolishly let my guard down. The bastards had snuck up on me.

There were four men all sitting around the fire, laughing and joking—almost the complete Pentagonal Coven, and I was to be there fifth. I shuddered at the thought.

There was a small snap as the binds around my hands broke.

"Don't move yet." Her hot breath was on my ear, sending tingles down my spine.

A burst of laughter came from the group of men, and I looked at them wide-eyed, willing them to ignore me like they had been doing for the past twenty minutes. I knew they had captured me to complete their circle. They had been boasting about it since I had been tied to this post, the arrogant sons of bitches.

"Okay. On my signal, we run," the woman hissed. It couldn't be wise to trust her, but what other option did I have? I did not want to stick around with these motherfuckers, and she did just free me.

"What signal?" I said as the last of my binds snapped around my neck and waist.

"You'll know," she said again, and I sneered at the men, hoping my rescuer had a better plan to incapacitate them than to just flee. They would follow with haste. I had been running from them for weeks and slipped up, which is when they finally snatched me up.

The fire started to crackle and hiss unnaturally, and then it fizzled out. Was that the signal? The men peered at it in concern, leaning over what once was a roaring pit of heat, now cold and docile.

Suddenly, the flames reignited in a blinding light of technicolor and latched onto each man like ropes as they howled in pain.

"*Run!*" the voice said behind me. I didn't waste any time as I shot up and sprinted after the dark figure into the depths of the forest.

I could hear cursing from where the men battled with the heat, but I focused on the woman in front of me. Her outline seemed to sparkle in the darkness, but I couldn't make out any features. I pumped my arms and legs fast to keep up, as I was not interested in what was left for me back at that camp.

Was she fae? They would often emit a glow, a glittery aura. Or perhaps a witch if she could control flames like that? Or even vampires by how swiftly and gracefully she moved? Possibly even a shifter if she was able to sneak around camp unnoticed.

In reality, it didn't matter. I didn't care as long as we got far away from my kidnappers.

A voice bellowed behind me, and I whipped my head around, not able to make out much more than vague shapes in the dark.

"Where are you, mortal? We worked so hard to become friends. We were just getting started," one of the men yelled, and laughter followed. Clearly, the flames did not keep them indisposed for too long

"Fuck." I looked around for my glittery new friend and saw nothing. Would she leave me out in the dark after freeing me?

A hissing ball of light appeared to my left through the shrubbery, swirling and expanding. It became so large, I could step through it—the woman stood on the other side of the circle.

A portal. She was opening a portal for us to escape.

She held out her gloved hand, and all I could make out were her bright gold eyes framed with thick lashes and a strip of dark brown skin.

"We don't have all day, princess. Let's go," she called. I could imagine her smirking underneath the cloth covering the lower part of her face.

I didn't need her to tell me twice. I ran to her, jumping into the portal just as I heard a voice behind me.

"A damn portal! Only a partial coven could have made that. FUCK!" he hollered, and I plunged into the gateway, colliding with my new friend as we tumbled together in a free fall.

I had never portaled before, and my head spun at a dizzying rate. I slammed eyes shut, begging the nausea to subside as I clung to my rescuer.

"Almost done, princess," she whispered into my ear, and my mouth went dry.

Her body felt good underneath mine—strong and steady where my hands clung, soft where I buried my face and sealed my eyes shut.

"Okay, princess, you can remove your face from my tits now. Not that I'm complaining, but you're safe. I'm Nayali, by the way, since now our bodies seem to be getting quite acquainted." Nayali looked down at me, and I realized I still hung on to her like a small child, my face indeed pressed between her breasts.

I jumped back quickly and swallowed hard, trying to hide my blush.

"Uh...sorry," I stuttered.

Nayali moved the cloth and smirked at me, revealing a small gap in her front teeth. Her lips were full, her head dusted in light brown curls cut close to her scalp.

"No need to apologize." She winked, and as she spoke, I noticed a glint of gold on her tongue. Was it pierced? An image of what it would feel like against my body flashed into my brain, and I told myself to settle down.

My nerves were fried, my body exhausted. I was feeling vulnerable and needy because I had been snatched by a group of males. It would be highly inappropriate to have those thoughts about the woman who just liberated me.

"Thank you, for saving me," I said, standing tall and squaring my shoulders as I finally looked around at my surroundings. We were transported in front of a large manor, firelight dancing alongside the towering iron door. It seemed like we were on top of a small hill, and the mansion overlooked it all.

"It's the least I could do, princess," she said, using that oddly intimate nickname again. I wasn't complaining; I just didn't know what to do with it. Nayali turned to the door, placing her palm on it as she whispered something I couldn't hear. It swung open, and she waved her hand out in front of her—an invitation to come inside.

"I'm not a princess," I said, walking slowly through the entryway.

"That's fine, but I don't know your name, and for some reason, I think that one suits you." The corners of her mouth tipped up, and we made our way through another set of doors. My stomach did an interesting flip flop that I tried to ignore so I could focus on what was in front of my face.

"Where are we? Do you live here?" I asked in awe as we stepped into a giant foyer. Stairs branched off in either direction, and a huge candlelit chandelier hung from the ceiling. A large banister loomed above us, another woman sitting precariously on the outside edge of it, eating an apple.

Her long black hair hung in a sheet to one side of her face, and tattoos snaked up her white skin and around her throat. She had bright ice blue eyes and light pink lips.

"I see you made it, Naya," she said, hopping off the banister and landing gracefully on the tiled floor—something no mortal could survive.

"Issa, this is our new friend," Nayali said as she began to unwind the many layers she had on, depositing knives, death stars, and various weaponry on a large round table in the middle of the entryway.

"What's your name, love?" Issa inquired, smiling softly.

"Hazel," I said. Issa barely wore any clothes: a simple band around her breasts and low hanging black pants with huge slits at the sides that seemed to billow with every movement. Tattoos covered her muscular body, and yet her voice was light and airy.

"Nice to meet you, Hazel. It looks like my portal worked just fine," she said, suddenly reaching for my hand.

"Thank you for using it on me... Well, for me..." I stammered. I had never seen anything like these two women before.

Nayali seemed to finally be content with herself—she stood in similar fashion. A top covered her breasts, and then tight, high waisted pants covering her curves, ending with black boots.

I swallowed, trying to get my hormones under control.

"Sure thing, Hazel. That's what magic is for," Issa said, leaning against the staircase to the left.

"You're both staring at the poor thing. Let's get her to a room to wash up, and then we will all have dinner." A third materialized from what felt like thin air behind me, and I whipped my head around. I stood in stunned silence. She was equally as threatening as she was beautiful, with wine colored hair that framed her face, red painted lips, and sea green eyes. Her skin was a light honey color, and she wore an outfit similar to the others. Her breasts were barely contained, and so much of her skin was daring to be touched. Her body was an endless dream of curves, rolls, and confidence.

I swallowed, trying not to stare too long before my belly started to do funny things again.

"You all have magic?" I said, electricity crackling in the air.

"Of course, darling, but we can chat more about this at dinner. You are safe here in our home. Do not worry—we are not like those brutes you saw before. Let us show you to your rooms, and we will answer all the questions you have at dinner," she soothed.

Issa reached for my hand and intertwined her fingers with mine.

"Come, Hazel. I will show you to your room for the evening." She dusted a kiss across my knuckles, and the sensation danced along my skin. Her hands were covered in beautiful ink, and I wondered what all lay beneath her billowy outfit.

"Okay," I whispered in return.

"'Scarlett, you nearly scared the shit out of her," I heard Nayali say as we walked up the stairs hand in hand.

"Sometimes I like to have a little fun, Naya." She laughed.

Issa pulled me along the never-ending corridors, and we arrived at a room that opened to a huge king sized bed, a vanity, and other luxuries I had never been permitted to have.

"I'll be back in 30 minutes to get you for dinner, alright? There are clothes in the vanity over there, and a bathroom through that door." She dusted a featherlight kiss on my cheek, and I tried not to blush.

"Thank you, Issa," I said, wanting to hold her lips against my cheek just a little bit longer.

"Of course, love," she said, as she seemingly danced away into the hallway.

My body was a bundle of nerves and in desperate need of soothing. I walked into the bathroom, where a large bath was already drawn, steam rising from the surface. Surely, this whole place wasn't magically gifted?

I stripped off my clothes and slid into the hot water with a loud exhale.

My whole body seemed to be simmering from the inside out. I needed to let off some of my own steam and find some sort of release. I looked around the bathroom, worried that someone might pop up out of nowhere, but I was alone. Carefully, I slung one leg out of the tub. I slid my fingers around my breasts and squeezed, needing to find a deeper release. I imagined Issa's mouth trailing featherlight kisses across my chest and then grabbed my nipples, picturing Scarlett's red mouth pulling and sucking at each one.

I moved my hand to my swollen clit, rubbing gently as I thought of Nayali's strong hands holding me while we portaled. I moaned, finding a rhythm that made my insides quiver and my thighs shake. I slipped my other hand down and pumped two fingers in and out of my swollen pussy, moving my hips for a bit more friction. An image popped into my mind of Scarlett and Issa on either breast, Nayali between my thighs, and I crashed into my orgasm.

Water splashed around me as I continued to circle my hips, riding each crest until I finally relaxed.

I cringed a little; it probably wasn't very proper to get off on being kidnapped, then saved and transported somewhere else with three stunningly powerful women, but I shook it off. It would be my little secret, something to get me through the night.

I climbed out of the tub and dried off. An outfit like theirs, just with a little more coverage, waited for me outside the bathroom: a cropped long sleeve with pants that only showed a sliver of my soft midsection.

I would have a good meal tonight and an even better sleep; then, I would figure out what the hell to do tomorrow morning.

A knock on the door interrupted my thoughts, and I walked over to answer it. It was someone I didn't recognize.

They had tanned skin and bleach blonde hair, streaks of purple laced throughout. Their features were sharp, their eyes purple. They sniffed at me and smiled.

"Oh, little one, no reason to be ashamed. We like to have all kinds of fun here."

I stood frozen in the doorway. Did they know I just had a spectacular orgasm thinking of everyone here?

"I'm Caro. Come; it's time for a different type of nourishment," they purred. I didn't know what else to do but follow along and hope I would survive this dinner.

Two

"Welcome, darling," Scarlett said from one side of an incredibly long table.

"I'll pour the wine," Nayali said, sweeping in. Issa was already seated and smiling sweetly.

"Do you feel better, love?" Issa's voice seemed to twinkle like a song.

"Yes, I do," I said shyly, hoping the others didn't know what Caro had seemingly known upon their arrival at my door. I sat down, twitching my fingers next to Issa, who gave my hand a light squeeze, sending tingles along my arm.

I looked down at the feast before us. Roasted meats, vegetables, rice, and fruits decorated the table. This was more than I had eaten in months. I had been on the run for so long, always stealing food and trying to sneak by others so as not to starve. My mouth watered at the sight.

"Don't be shy, Hazel. Eat up," Caro said, sitting on the other side of me, Nayali across from me next to Scarlett.

"Why?" I said, needing to know this wasn't a trap. I had been taken advantage of before, and I didn't want that to happen to me here.

Men had tried to recruit me to finish their coven, and I always refused. I didn't know what magic would trap me, and I certainly couldn't offer myself to them physically. The thought of being with them wasn't something that particularly got my blood hot.

What little I knew of completing a Pentagonal Coven came from rumors and what I had overhead from groups that had tried to approach me. They never explained anything or told me what was going on. They would go straight for group sex, and I would flee because I didn't know what else to do. They used coercion and manipulation that terrified me as a mortal.

"Why what, Hazel?" Nayali asked, sipping on wine.

"Why did you help me? Are you trying to force me into your coven like everyone else? Because I won't do it. I won't sacrifice myself for people I don't know and things I don't understand," I clarified, trying not to let my voice quiver.

"You needed help, so I helped," Nayali replied, like it could just be that simple.

"So you don't want anything from me?" I asked skeptically, looking around at each of them.

"I wouldn't say we don't want anything," Caro said with a wink, and I blushed while squeezing my thighs together.

"Car!" Issa scolded.

"We don't expect anything in return for helping you. Saul's partial coven is a nasty gang, and they have been trying to trap a mortal woman for years. They deal in primitive magic. A coven is supposed to be consensual and loving, but it turns dark when violence and assault are involved. A coven should be a haven of love and support, not one based on fear and force," Scarlett spat.

"Saul kidnapped our beloved Angelica," Issa muttered sadly.

"Don't, Issa," Scarlett pleaded.

"It's important Hazel knows she can trust us," she replied, folding her tattooed hands over each other on the table.

"Angelica was our fifth point," Nayali explained.

"So you are—or were—a coven, then?" I asked quietly.

"Yes, but we have been incomplete since Saul kidnapped Angelica and killed her," Nayali hissed. "He took our beloved, and she ran. He's a shifter, and he changed while hunting her, but he could not control his beast. He tore her to shreds."

"This happened several years ago, and since then, we have kept an eye on him and his brothers in an effort to protect those who may fall prey to his violence," Caro said, fury in their eyes.

"Why not just kill them then?" I wondered.

"We have tried many times but have never succeeded." Scarlett's eyes misted over, and her mouth formed a thin line.

"Losing your fifth point, especially the one who fills the role of your beloved, is incredibly devastating. It's like losing a chunk of your heart. It's exhausting to recover from," Issa said, stroking my arm sadly, sending electricity skittering across my skin.

"I don't fully understand how completed covens work. I have been approached many times, mainly by covens full of men. They usually try to intimidate and seduce me right away, and I flee. It's what I've been doing with Saul and his group, but they finally caught up to me." It was hard to focus with Issa's stroking fingertips, but I wanted to know. No longer would I be kept in the dark.

"Let us explain it to you then," Caro said. "A complete pentagonal coven is rare and beautiful. It is a bond shared between fie individuals. A witch like Scarlett. A vampire like Nayali. A fae like Issa. A shifter like me. And a mortal like you." They flashed a silky smile my way, and I tried not to let the fluttering in my lower belly show.

"Calm down, Car. Don't scare poor Hazel away," Scarlett

drawled. "When five of these beings join, there can be a large ascent of power. The mortal is the most important being in the coven because they have no magic; they become a conductor of sorts to link all the others together. The strongest covens create a link with their beloved mortal emotionally and physically through a ritual."

"What do you mean, *create a link emotionally and physically*?" I said, trying not to squirm in my seat as heat went straight to my thighs. I needed my libido to keep it together.

"The mortal must accept the other beings consensually through a sexual ritual to ascend to the highest access of shared power. The other beings essentially vow not to have any relation outside of their beloved mortal, and the mortal agrees to love the other four equally. It is meant to give power to the mortal, who was not born with magical or otherworldly power. The stronger your love is, the stronger the magic. It turns dark and dangerous when love isn't involved. It can be downright deadly."

I swallowed, trying not to think of how things could have gone awry in previous situations when I had been approached aggressively.

"I saved you not because our intention was to recruit you, but because you need someone to support you," Nayali said softly.

"But what if I was interested?" I said before I realized it left my mouth. I had never wanted to join a coven before, but something about theirs called to me like a string to my heart. Now that I understood more, my interest was piqued.

"What?" Caro said, snapping their head to look at me with a sparkle in their eyes.

"What if I was interested in completing your coven?" I asked again, a little louder.

"We can't replace Angelica," Scarlett snapped.

"We aren't replacing her, Scar. We are moving through the grief process," Issa replied.

"What if we tried on a trial basis?" Nayali inquired, sitting back in her chair.

"I need to think about this." Scarlett pushed from the table and stomped away.

"I didn't mean to insert myself. I don't want to cause trouble after all you have done, but I've never wanted to try with another group before. You all ignite something in me, and I would be interested in trying it out," I said seriously. I was tired of running. I had no family and no resources. If they were willing to try with me, I was sure I could rise to the occasion.

"I'll talk with her, little one," Caro said, running a hand along my thigh. I tried not to shiver.

"Okay," I whispered.

"In the meantime, you need your strength. Eat up, princess." Nayali winked and dove right in. I ate in silence for the rest of my meal. Scarlett never came back, and it was oddly hurtful, despite us meeting hours ago. Issa finally led me back to my room, and I tried to get more familiar with the maze of the house.

"Tomorrow, we can do a tour and talk about what we've decided. We're a family, Hazel. We do not share our powers and our bodies lightly, but I believe there's a reason we found you and you, us," Issa said.

"It honestly was a silly idea. I've never asked to be a part of a coven before, and I guess I really don't understand what it means. I feel, um...connected to all of you in some shape or form," I said, rubbing my arms.

"Does connected mean attracted to, love?" Issa teased, smiling slyly.

I bit my lip and giggled.

"Yes. I mean, you all are stunning, and I would be lying if I said I wasn't interested in what our bodies could share," I said, feeling heat pool low and spread to my inner thighs.

Issa came in closer, running her fingertips along my arms.

"Trust me, love, we're all interested as well. There aren't many all femme covens. We hold a special kind of power that can be accessed when we all commit."

"I wouldn't want to be in one like Saul's," I whispered as Issa's fingertips started to play with my long ponytail.

"Tonight, when you touch yourself, I want you to think of me leaving my mark on you," she said in my ear, and I shivered, my panties growing wet.

"Your mark?" I asked.

"Yes," she purred. "Some could say it's my kink. Love bites, lip stains, tattoos; I want to see myself on your skin. Imagine my lips leaving permanent marks in their wake, my teeth little love bites." Her tongue darted out to lick the shell of my ear, and I nearly fell over.

"Now, go play with yourself, and don't be afraid to be loud, love. I'm sure it's a lovely thing to hear." Then, she slipped away, her pants billowing around her strong thighs.

"I shut the door quickly and slid my hands down to my clit, which was already aching from her instructions. I didn't even make it to the bed as I circled my center, pumping two fingers in and out as I groaned a throaty moan.

I hoped it pleased Issa, because even though I could touch myself all day long, what I really wanted was for her to use that wicked tongue and brand me with her lips.

THREE

"Princess, it's time to rise and shine." Nayali ran her fingertips across my cheek.

My eyes shot open, and I tried to ignore the blush creeping across my skin. "Is this how you wake everyone up?"

"Only you. Just seeing if there's a spark here, you know?" she said, smiling and folding her legs onto the bed, facing me.

"Right. Does that mean I get a trial run?" I asked hopefully. I had thought about it after I had done what I needed to do for my body. I wanted to be safe and loved. Maybe this was where that could happen? If not loved, at least protected and cherished.

"Scarlett agreed, but you'll have to do some work to win her over. Don't worry; today, we'll show you around and answer any questions you have. Then, we will start the trial by spending time with you one-on-one to decide if we all agree. If everyone finds they want you to be a part of this coven and you the same, we will move forward with the formal ritual of sharing power. It can be pretty intense, both physically and emotionally, so we will do our best to prepare you," Nayali said, leaning back on her hands.

"That sounds reasonable. I still want to do this—or at least try," I said, standing up and reaching for the robe I had discovered in the wardrobe the night before.

"The coven is meant to be magical for everyone, physically and emotionally. You have nothing to worry about in terms of your safety or doing anything you don't want to do. However, we will ask for your clear and open consent. We each have tastes that can make all things fun to explore, but we expect everyone to be clear about their boundaries," Nayali said, watching me closely as I grabbed a brush and tried to work through my tangly waves.

"I promise I can communicate what I need and will expect you all to do the same," I said, nodding and sitting down in front of the mirror. Nayali came up behind me and grabbed the brush from my hands.

"May I?" she asked.

"Sure," I replied, swallowing.

She started to brush the tangles out, her fingertips skittering across my neck and scalp. I tried not to moan at how good it felt to have her hands in my hair.

"Do you like this, princess?" she whispered into my ear. My cheeks heated at her words.

"Yes." I watched as she continued to brush my hair and maintain eye contact with me. Slowly, she set the brush down.

"How do you feel about hair pulling?" she whispered in my ear.

"What do you mean?" I said, breathless.

"It can add a fun layer of pleasure, princess. Can I show you?" she asked seriously. "All you have to say is enough if you're not into it."

"I've never had anyone do it for pleasure... I've had men try as a way to control me."

"This is meant to be for you, princess, and for me. A mutual moment of trust and care. I want both of us to feel good, and I want you to trust me," Nayali said.

"Okay, I trust you," I said. And I did. Nayali saved me when she didn't have to, and I'd been given every opportunity to leave whenever I wanted.

Nayali started massaging my scalp and then gently palmed my skull with a slight tug so my head moved to the side. My dark brown hair fell, exposing my neck. I gave a little gasp as the power slipped from my grip and into hers. It felt good to have someone take control in a way that I knew wouldn't hurt me.

Nayali smiled as I closed my eyes. "Open your eyes, princess. I want to show you something."

Obeying, I opened my eyes and saw the olive skin on my neck was exposed, right underneath Nayali's lips.

"Yes, Nayali," I whined.

She smiled, and then two pointed fangs elongated from her gums.

I gasped as she scraped her pointed teeth along my skin.

"You really are a vampire," I said as fluttering began in my stomach. I thought of how it would feel to have her teeth sink into my skin. I imagined it would be hot, electric.

"Yes. I won't bite you today, princess, but I will if we decide to move forward and share our powers with you." She darted her tongue out and licked where my shoulder met my neck, her grip pulling a little harder on my hair. Heat went straight to my thighs as I wiggled and gasped underneath her.

"Now, Nayali. We aren't playing just yet," Caro said from the doorway with a smirk.

"Car, you ruined my fun," Nayali said into my skin and gently rubbed my scalp with a featherlight kiss on my shoulder.

"We need to let Hazel get ready for the tour, which will

begin with me, seeing as you've already stolen some time with our lovely guest," they said.

"Fine, but let's give Hazel a moment to herself before we begin," Nayali conceded, dragging Caro out with her.

"I will be back for you, little one, and I'll show you just a wink of what this life could be." With that, they were both out the door, and I was left to myself, wondering what exactly I was getting myself into.

———

"Can I ask you something, Caro?" I said as we walked along the corridors of the mansion.

"Sure thing, little one. I'm an open book. You can call me Car," they replied.

"Okay, Car. Tell me about Angelica, and how she fit in. Will I constantly be compared to her? Is that why Scarlett is so upset about me trying to make this work?" I nibbled on my thumb, wanting to know all the details.

"Angelica felt like our miracle," they said, sighing and stopping at one of the lush furnishings and sat down. I did the same.

"Your miracle?"

"As I am sure you may have put together, there are not many all femme covens. It's much more likely that your coven is mixed or all men with one woman, so to find someone who was also femme who wanted to be with us felt like the stars had aligned," Caro said, crossing their legs over one another and leaning back into the plush velvet seat.

"How did you all find one another in the first place?" I wondered how covens even formed.

"A lot of families tend to have relations with other magical families and will hold parties to introduce their children to children with other gifts. It's mutually beneficial to have at least one child join a coven and the rest further the family line."

I nodded, waiting for them to continue.

"We ended up meeting in various ways. Scarlett was on the run, and Nayali met up with her, as her eldest brother had already joined a coven. Issa and I met at one of our family's parties and then decided to go out because we didn't want to share power with any men. Then, we finally all ran into one another rescuing mortals from different all men covens." Car leaned forward, their head in their hand.

"Angelica was one of those we rescued who asked if she could try and join. We had others ask, but none we said yes to. We said yes to her, and it was a fit. Something made sense with all of us together. You give off a similar but different spark, little one. Scarlett has her own demons and felt especially seen by Angelica, so it was extremely hard on all of us when we lost her. We never thought we would feel for another but something about you is making some of us hopeful. I think that scares Scar."

"Do you think she would talk to me about it if I gained her trust?" I wondered how I could get her to open up to me.

"I think she would, little one. Just be patient." Caro squeezed my knee, and I shuddered. Claws started to elongate from Car's fingertips.

"Shifter magic," I breathed as the claws gently scraped my skin. The sharpness of the pain sent pleasure up my thighs.

"Do you like the claws, little one?" Caro said, biting a little deeper into my skin.

"Yes," I breathed.

"Interesting. We will play soon, but not yet," Caro said, and I let out a breath when their claws left my skin, the warmth of their hand disappearing from my body.

With those words, Caro reached for my fingers and guided me along the rest of the tour. I tried not to think too much of what it would mean to live up to someone who made the stars align.

FOUR

"Are you ready for your first trial, darling?" Scarlett said, her arms crossed, looking at me expectantly.

Caro had been showing me around, and they said today, we would go through the first intimate trial. I was ready to do whatever they wanted, eager to please them. This felt like where I needed to be and who I needed to be with, even though Scarlett still intimated me.

"I'm ready," I said, determined to get her to like me, maybe even treat me like their once-beloved.

"Follow me then." Scarlett led me down several sets of stairs, and we entered a room I had not been shown yet. It felt like a dungeon, and I tried not to think about what that could mean. It was simultaneously arousing and terrifying.

We stopped in front of a large metal door, and she waved her hand in front of it. With a creak, it swung open to reveal a large, open space.

There was a table in the middle of the room, where Issa, Caro, and Naya already sat. There was a tub in front of the fireplace, steaming from the heat. Several plush chairs and pillows sat around the room alongside a few low tables. The space was littered with food, beverages, and some odd looking tools I was unfamiliar with.

"Hazel!" Issa's eyes lit up, and I relaxed a bit. Issa's smiles were like a warm hug.

"Princess," Nayali greeted. Her fangs popped out as she licked her lips. The image of her behind me this morning popped into my head, sending heat between my thighs. I could still feel the lap of her tongue up my neck.

"Little one," Caro said, blowing a kiss at me. They each seemed to have a special name for me, and it made my heart flutter. It was like each of them gave me a little piece of them, even Scarlett.

"Let's go over there." Scarlett guided me over to one of the tables with the interesting tools. "Do you know what some of these are, darling?"

"Um, I think I could guess about some, but others, I'm not sure. I don't understand why they are all together." I twirled a piece of hair around my finger as I gazed at the spread.

"Well, if you're to be the fifth piece of our coven, specifically the one we share our bodies with, we each have specific tastes." She stroked some of the items lovingly.

"These are our toys," Caro said, walking up to stand beside Scarlett.

"Toys to play with? With me?" I said, not sure I knew exactly what she meant. I had been with people of all genders before, but I had never used any toys or tools. It was usually a rushed night, with drinks and minimal talking. There wasn't often much to discuss besides getting one another off. This was something completely new to me.

"Yes, love. We each have things we like, and part of the acceptance of this coven is understanding and wanting to engage with some of those things. We want to understand your tastes too." Issa's fingers brushed my arm with each word. I shivered and nodded.

"Okay. So what do you all like to play with?" I asked, looking at the array of things with a newfound curiosity.

"Well, princess, you know I like to do a little bit of hair pulling and light choking. I also enjoy collaring, which means I would put something like this around your pretty throat and use it to tell you where I want you to be and when." Nayali picked up a leather necklace with a round metal ring attached to it.

I pictured it on my skin, Nayali pulling me close by the metal with just a little force. The thought got me excited and made my clit start to ache. The image of Nayali using it to guide me with a firm hand down to her pussy and what might lie there for me made my mouth water.

"So you like it, princess?" Nayali asked, smiling and flicking her tongue out. I saw her piercing again. God, I wanted to know how that cold metal would feel against my hot center.

"Yes, I would want to try that." Confidence and lust bloomed within me. I had never had anyone ask for something else besides basic sex and the thought thrilled me.

"I like marking or branding, love," Issa said, picking up something that looked like a needle and another that looked like a stamp. "It's a delicate balance between pleasure and pain, Hazel. It shows everyone you belong to this coven. We can make them permanent, or we can make them temporary, but I like to leave marks to show what's mine," Issa said in her soft voice. It was like a song that called to me, and the thought of her doing whatever she wanted with my body made me squirm.

"I trust you would make it feel good, that it would stoke a fire in me," I said, meaning it. I already felt something between us. The urge to please her was strong, to let her do whatever she wanted.

"Little one, I like to do something a little more...penetrative," Caro said, grabbing something that looked very similar to a penis.

"Okay," I said, waiting for them to continue as I squeezed my inner thighs.

"I can strap this to me and use it in any of your holes. Have you ever had someone in your ass, little one?" Caro asked gently.

"Yes, but never like that. It felt different, but in a good way, like a deeper orgasm that I definitely want to try again." Car's controlled excitement made my chest warm. I wanted to feel what they could give me and relish in being in their control.

"That's good, little one. That's very good," Caro whispered, their voice hoarse.

I looked at Scarlett expectantly, as there were multiple things on the table no one had spoken to. I knew she would be last.

"I'm a pleasure domme, darling," Scarlett said, gauging my reaction. I didn't have one.

"I don't know what that is," I said self-consciously.

"It means I get off when you get off...again, again, and again. So, I will use all the toys to make you scream my name, and you will do as I say, or I will torture you with never ending pleasure." She smirked, putting her hands on her hips.

"And we all like to watch," Caro added, grabbing my hand and leading me over to the fireplace and the tub.

"The first trial, darling, is showing us what you like," Scarlett said.

"You were quite active in the tub before, and we would like to see you do it again, love. Then, we will see it with one of our toys," Issa whispered in my ear. My whole body lit up with goosebumps.

"Okay." Slowly, I stripped off my clothes. Naya's eyes lit up when my top came off, and I squeezed my nipples while maintaining eye contact with her.

"You have fantastic tits, princess. I can't wait to put them in my mouth," Naya said, her fangs extending. My panties flooded with moisture as I slid my pants off. Moving one foot out and then the other, I exposed myself to them. Issa looked longingly at me.

"Oh yes, love. I will have to brand that plump ass of yours," she said, biting her lip.

"I can smell your pussy dripping from here, little one, and it's making me ravenous," Caro commented.

Scarlett said nothing as she watched me slide into the tub, the water right at my nipple line.

"Now touch yourself, darling, and show us how you come undone." It was a command, one I had no interest in disobeying. She waived her hand, and four different chairs appeared around the tub as they all sat back to watch me.

There was something powerful about having all the attention on me, their innate desire to see me pleasure myself. It was something I could get high from, and it made my pussy ache even more.

"We're waiting, princess," Naya said, sliding her own hand down to her pants.

I nodded and reached for the body soap on the side. I lathed my hands to start to massage and knead my own breasts. My fingertips played with my nipples, and I groaned. My hips swayed in the water on their own, my body already needing more friction.

"Yes, little one. Pull at those big, beautiful tits of yours," Caro said hungrily.

I moved my hands down to my achy center, and they all

scooted closer to watch my hand circled my swollen clit. My other hand slowly made its way to my entrance, and in one quick motion, I sheathed my finger inside.

"Add another, darling. Don't be shy," Scarlett ordered, her eyes glowing. It was the first thing she had said, and I wanted to please her. So, I added a second one as I pumped in out of my pussy and circled my clit. The heat inside me roared with each stroke of my fingers.

"Another one?" I asked, looking to Scarlett for permission.

"See, she already wants to please you, Scar." Issa looked pleased. Scarlett nodded and cleared her throat.

"Yes, darling. I give you permission to add another." I added a third finger and pumped only twice before I came undone, moaning as water sloshed around me. My nipples perked up out of the water. I rode my hand, grinding against my fingers until the pleasure was all gone. My eyes popped open; I didn't even realize I had squeezed them shut.

"Next time, your gaze will be on us so we can see the pleasure in your big, beautiful brown eyes," Issa said, pulling my hand to hers and sucking on one of the fingers that was once inside me. I nearly came again at the sensation.

Caro grabbed my hand and sucked another finger, Nayali the other.

Scarlett snatched the other hand touching my clit and licked it clean. My pussy clenched again, and liquid started to seep out of me.

"Your clit is so sweet, darling," she said, and I stood.

"No more playing tonight. We will start tomorrow. A trial with each of us, and then, if you pass, the group ritual will begin." She left without another word, her hips swaying.

Issa helped me out of the tub as Caro grabbed a towel for me.

"You did good, princess. So tasty and eager," Nayali said.

She walked me back to my bedchamber and grazed my cheek with a chaste kiss goodnight.

I was stunned. I had never been a part of something like that, and I felt full and hungry for more. There was power in being a part of a group like this. The more time I spent with them, the more I realized I wanted to be their fifth point. I would be what they needed and wanted, and they surely would do the same for me.

FIVE

"Good morning, love." Issa was lying beside me as I woke up and blinked sleep out of my eyes. She was lovingly stroking my arms, and it sent tingles along my skin.

"Hi," I said sleepily. This was a wonderful way to wake up.

There was something calm and inherently loving about Issa. I immediately felt like I could be myself with her, and I wanted to just soak in her energy.

"Today is our day together," she whispered across my cheek. Her curtain of black hair was tied back into a simple braid, her tattoos on full display.

"Can I ask a question, Issa?" I asked. Her lips were inches away from mine.

"Yes, love," she said, pulling back to look at me.

"Will you tell me about your tattoos?"

She smiled like she had a secret. Her laugh twinkled, and she settled beside me, patting her thigh. I laid my head there, and her fingers twisted through my tangled strands as she answered my question.

"I'm fae, and in my family, it's tradition to choose markings that tell your story. I wanted to embrace femininity and the power that comes with it. The flowers are mixed with weapons and pictures of feminine divinity. I like to get a new one every time I go through a large life event, so maybe I'll get one when you're officially inducted into the coven. I did with Angelica," she replied thoughtfully, looking at a five pointed star on the back of her hand with thorns and roses on it.

"That is, if everyone accepts me," I said, feeling unsure. My focus fractured as she continued to run her fingers along my scalp.

"Don't worry, love. You will. Everyone just needs time to get to know and understand you." Her words were so sure, like she already knew this was going to work out, even though I was anxious it wouldn't. My eyes found hers and then dipped to her lips. I couldn't help but wonder what she would taste like.

"Do you want me to kiss you, love?" Her voice practically caressed my skin.

I sat up and nodded, facing her.

"Lay back," she commanded softly, and I obeyed.

I set myself up against my headboard, and she gently climbed on top of me. Her muscular legs encased my hips, and my breath caught in my throat. She moved my hair away from my eyes, brushing her fingertips along my temples and collarbone. I shivered as her touch sent heat to my low belly.

"Can I mark you today, Hazel?" she asked.

I nodded again, unable to say anything, absolutely transfixed by her commanding confidence.

She grabbed my hand and licked the skin on the inside of my wrist, my mouth opened in a little o. Issa brought her lips to the space she just licked, and heat seared my skin as she kissed the delicate pulse there. I groaned as she pulled away, and there were her lips, marked on my wrist.

I gasped.

"A little bit of fae magic. I control energy. Portals, some temperature manipulation, and enhanced physical abilities. We can explore what all that means later, as our day is just getting started." She ground her hips against my center, and I yelped.

"Issa, please," I said, wanting to finally taste her lips. The teasing was killing me, and I wanted desperately to know what her hot mouth would feel against my own.

"As you wish, Hazel," she said seductively, like the idea had been hers all along.

She brought her lips to mine and brushed them oh so slightly. Just a touch. A wonderful, terrible tease.

I groaned, and she pushed into me, pressing her whole body and mouth against mine. I arched my back, and her tongue slipped through the seam of my lips. Her body felt so right on top of mine. She grabbed my chin and forced my mouth open even more before she dove in.

Her tongue danced in between my lips, and I sucked hard, grinding my hips into hers as my pussy throbbed and ached with every swipe of her tongue. She left my mouth and branded me with her lips at the base of my neck. I gasped as the heat exploded across my skin.

Issa pulled back, looking pleased with herself.

"Now you have two marks from me, love. We will make sure to give you a few more before I leave you today. There is so much more to explore." She slipped her hand down and found my panties wet.

"So you like this so far, Hazel?" she asked, a twinkle in her eye. She grabbed my hand and slid it into her own panties. I gasped as I touched her wet folds.

"You like this too? You like me?" I said, feeling her wetness and gently circling her swollen clit. She ground against me, smiling wickedly.

"Oh, yes, I like you very much." She slipped her hand out

of my arousal and grabbed my hand, intertwining our fingers and mixing our essence. It was erotic to see our palms damp with another's essence.

"Let's get you dressed and ready to go." She pulled me in for one more searing kiss. She thrust her tongue into my mouth boldly while I sucked it, feeling needy for more of her touch.

Issa pulled away and climbed off me, dragging me to stand.

"Go, love." She swatted my ass and bit her lip as I giggled and walked away.

I could do this. Issa stirred something in me sexually and emotionally that was both terrifying and lovely. I wanted to dive into her layers as much as I wanted her to dive into mine. I couldn't wait for our day to begin, so I hustled to get dressed and let my excitement bloom through my body with each breath I took.

———

"Tell me why you wanted to do this, Hazel, especially after all those bad experiences," Issa asked. We had traveled outside the manor to the surrounding woods, where we had a picnic. We had spent the afternoon feeding each other little bits of food in between laughter and light touches.

"Truthfully, partly because of you," I responded shyly.

"Me?" Issa seemed delighted.

"Yes. You just make me feel seen and comfortable in a way I didn't know I needed. I feel safe with you, like you're holding me in your hands. You won't let anything bad happen to me," I said, genuinely meaning it. Things were easy with Issa. She was beautiful, strong, and uniquely herself.

"I think you deserve a kiss for that, love," she said brightly.

Her lips met mine, and sparks flew again, wet heat pooling low as my belly began to flutter.

"Why did you decide to let me try this?" I said between kisses, never wanting to let her lips go. She pulled back and studied me.

"Something about you called to me as well. You have a light that beckons to me. Our coven needs that after what happened with Angelica. You also smell like sugar cookies, and I really can't resist it," she teased.

"Thank you, Issa."

"Of course, Hazel. Shall we continue our day? I want to show you some of what my fae sense can do besides smelling that you're ready for something else." She winked at me, and I gasped.

"You can smell my arousal?" I gasped, squeezing my inner thighs.

"Yes. I can also feel your pulse quicken, and I notice the small movements of your body. It's not easy to hide those things from me. I have the gift of energy flow from my generational gifts as well as portal making. I'll show you," She reached her tattooed hands out, and it was like the air around them changed. Electricity sizzled around us while a portal began to open and expand to my bedroom. She sent heat in my direction, and I felt it whisper across my body.

She closed her palms, and the portal and the warmth disappeared.

"Wow, Issa. You're extraordinary," I said in awe.

"I want to portal you to somewhere special, Hazel. Is that alright?" she asked.

"I trust you." I nodded my head and wondered where she could possibly be taking me.

She opened another portal, smoke in the dark shadows. I couldn't make out where we were going. Issa gestured with her hand for me to grab. I latched on to it and immediately felt calm.

We tumbled through the portal together, Issa's strong arms stabilizing me as I closed my eyes until the spinning stopped.

"You can open your eyes, love. We're here," she said.

I opened them and looked around. We were in a bedroom with a huge blood red satin bed, candles littering the entire space. Rose petals tumbled around, and a fire roared in the corner.

"Is this your bedroom?" I asked, in awe of the luxurious fabrics, colors, and heat.

"Yes, love, and we're about to see just how compatible our bodies are with one another," she said, leading me to the bed and slowly pushing me down to sit.

"Are you ready, Hazel?" she asked in a low purr.

"I'm ready," I exclaimed. I wanted Issa, and she wanted me. I was ready to be consumed by her power.

"Then let's begin."

Six

"We'll have a safe word today, Hazel. Can you pick one for me? When you say it, it means we will pause and decide whether to continue or stop and decompress. Do you understand?" Issa asked, standing in front of me while I sat on her satin bed.

"Yes, I understand." I nodded, knowing this was all to keep me safe.

"What word would you like to use?" she asked, letting her hair fall partially in her face as she gently undid her braid.

"Pink?" I asked, trying to think of any scenario where I would use that while playing.

"Great. Pink it is." Issa beamed at me, and my face started to heat. "Here's what I would like to do today, love. I like biting and branding as well as temperature play. Do you think you would want to explore one of those things, all of them, or none of them?" She put her hands on my knees and pressed into me as I leaned back, transfixed by her eyes.

"I would like to try all of them, Issa. I trust you," I said, growing excited and wet.

"Okay, love. Let's start with both of us getting naked.

Can I undress you?" she asked softly. I didn't have words as I nodded silently. She grabbed my hands and helped me stand.

She gave me a light kiss, and my eyes fluttered closed. Her lips were like a zap of electricity sending tingles toward my center. Issa started to gently trail her mouth with the lightest of pressure across my skin as she carefully exposed my breasts and slid off my pants.

Her lips seemed to be everywhere at once, heat and pressure blooming in her wake. I gasped, realizing her touch was heated from her lips to her fingertips to every brush of her skin.

I was naked in no time at all. She cupped my cheeks and pulled me in for a deeper kiss that nearly had me exploding with pleasure. Her tongue gently explored my mouth, and I wanted more of her and her delicious sensations.

"Issa," I whimpered, and she grinned against my lips.

"Lay back, love," she responded. Issa gently pushed me back to the bed and started to undress herself while maintaining eye contact. She released the band around her breasts and slid her billowy pants off. Her body was strong and beautiful. Muscles and tattoos wrapped around her whole being. She moved with grace and precision as she climbed on top of me.

"Issa, you're stunning," I mumbled, not knowing what to say. I wanted to trace each tattoo with my tongue.

"You'll get your turn to, love. This is an exchange of pleasure, and you get to do whatever you want without shame or judgement. First, though, I will show you what it means to be cared for," she said, sitting on my hips. I could feel her wetness, and mine started to seep down my thighs.

"Close your eyes, love, and relax," she whispered. Her hair tickled my skin, and I shuddered.

I tried to simply tune in to her words and my senses.

"First, I'll add a little cold," she whispered, and I gave a little nod.

Her mouth was like ice as it licked and caressed my nipples until they peaked and ached. I gasped as the sensation quickly turned from freezing to searing warmth. The change in temperature had me rubbing my thighs together and moaning.

"How does that feel, love?" Issa chuckled.

"So good. The temperature change is like nothing I've ever felt," I breathed, and her fingertips started to trail my body, exploring with sharp coldness before drastically changing to a boiling touch. I was squirming and wiggling underneath her, and we had just gotten started.

"I'm going to add to our temperature game, love. I'm going to brand you with my lips and fingertips. Is that okay? It will be like a quick burn," she said.

"Yes. Do it."

Her fingertips turned searing as they danced across my nipples and hips before her lips branded my breast. I gasped as her mouth pressed into my skin, and a blast of cold breath followed. My eyes opened to see her hovering over my aching nipples.

"How'd that feel, love?" she asked, and I bubbled with joy.

"Like I might orgasm from that alone. Can you do it again?" I was soaking into her sheets at this point, practically panting.

"Your wish is my command, love," she said. Issa made her way down my body, biting and tattooing her lips and teeth across my whole being. The pleasure inside me started to crest higher as I rubbed my own nipples, fighting the urge to grind my hips into her beautiful body.

She settled over the apex of my thighs and spread me wide.

"Oh, you smell delicious, love," Issa said, blowing cold air across my clit. I gasped and squirmed, it sent sensations straight down my inner thighs. She did it once more, and I moaned, arching my spine.

"Please, Issa," I begged. She dove right in with her hot tongue, lapping and kissing at my center. My first orgasm crashed into me, and I yelled her name like a prayer.

"Again, love," she commanded as she went back in on my aching clit. My body was over-sensitized to every temperature change and pressure she applied. Her fingers began to gently push through my wet folds and curl into a spot that had me riding another wave of ecstasy. I cried out again, convulsing and shaking as my orgasm racked my body.

"On your stomach, love," Issa commanded, and I flipped over. She pulled my ass up and branded each of my cheeks. I gasped as her fingertips dug into my hips.

She started to eat me out from behind, and I whined as my face pressed deeper into her satin sheets. Another orgasm ripped through me, and my thighs clenched around her.

"Issa!" I screamed as I rode my waves of pleasure.

"Hazel, love," she said, flipping me over and bringing her lips to mine. I could taste myself on her, and it made me ravenous for my turn.

"Can I taste you, Issa? Please?" I begged, wanting to know what her pleasure tasted like on my tongue.

"Yes, love. Are you feeling satisfied with your own plea-sure?" she asked.

"Yes, Issa." I scrambled up to get a better look at her.

"I want to trace your tattoos with my tongue." I licked my lips while I made a slow perusal of her on the sheets.

"Put that tongue to use then," she said with a smirk.

So, I went to work, moving along the lines of her body with my mouth and wringing out every gasp and shiver I could from her. I moved across her nipples, sucking greedily at each one. It made my own wetness build and creep down my thighs.

Issa touched herself as I moved along her body, and it was glorious to see her pull her own pleasure with her fingers, married with my tongue and mouth dancing across her beautiful skin.

She groaned and gasped as an orgasm pushed through her. I sucked her breasts while she rode it out on her fingertips. Once she finished, I grabbed her hand and licked her digits clean, already addicted to the taste of her.

"Issa, will you sit on my face please?" The only thing I could think of was more. More of her. More of us. It was a craving building underneath my skin and flooding my veins.

"Yes, love, I think I can do that." She pushed me down and placed a pillow underneath my neck. When she looked satisfied with my setup, she straddled my lips, her hands on her headboard.

I could smell her, the wetness glistening on her pretty folds.

"Are you ready for me?" she asked seductively, and I licked my lips in response.

She lowered herself onto me, and I was engulfed by her essence. My hands immediately went to the globes of her ass. All I could think of was having my way with her swollen clit. She tasted so good. I hungrily lapped and sucked at her center. Her hips thrust against me, riding my face as my own orgasm started to build in my body in tune with hers. Her groans, and the movement of her pelvis had me reaching down to play with myself while my tongue moved inside her.

I gasped as my own orgasm pushed through me, and I latched on to her thighs, plunging my tongue deeper, chasing my own release to crash into hers. Issa moaned and grabbed at her breasts, pulling at her nipples.

"Hazel!" she yelled. I continued to lap and suck at her quivering pussy.

Her pace began to slow, and she gently moved off me. She placed a sloppy kiss on my lips.

"You're beautiful with my cum all over your face, Hazel." Her face held a look of pure satisfaction.

I giggled as she lay down next to me, and we intertwined our bodies, our faces inches apart.

"Issa, I've never had sex like that in my entire life," I whispered against her lips. The smell of our passion and pleasure mixed between us to create something uniquely ours. It was sensational.

"Did it feel good? Do you feel desired, love?" She moved my hair away from my eyes.

"I do. Did I do okay with you? I haven't had sex with someone in a long time." I suddenly felt a little self-conscious. Clearly, Issa knew what she was doing. I hoped I lived up to her expectations.

"You were exactly what I wanted and needed, Hazel." She kissed the tip of my nose, and we snuggled into one another.

My eyes started to drift closed, and I heard her whisper, "You're the fifth we've been looking for, love. You're perfect exactly the way you are."

Sleep overtook me, and I dreamed of Issa's body on top of mine and the many orgasms we traded between us.

SEVEN

"You all look cozy and cute," Nayali cooed at us. I woke up tangled in Issa's arms, and she grinned at me.

"It's Nayali's turn to show you who she is. Go on, love. I will see you soon." Issa dusted a light kiss on my forehead, then nose, then mouth. I squeezed her tight and sat up, looking at Naya's smiling face.

"Did you two have a fun night?" She sniffed the air like she already knew. "Smells like sex." Naya licked her lips, and I fought a blush growing on my cheeks. I saw the flash of her tongue piercing again, and my belly quivered.

"Stop your teasing, Naya. You're making Hazel blush!" Issa laughed, lounging on the bed.

"Come on, princess. Let's get you cleaned up." Nayali flashed her teeth again, and I let her pull me up. She handed me a robe, and I pulled it around myself.

"Bye Issa." I waved as I exited her room.

"Bye, love."

Nayali led me back to my room and walked me over to the

bathroom. Tenderly, she untied my robe and slipped the fabric off, her fingertips trailing along my arms.

"You are stunning, Hazel. Do you know that?" I tried not to blush again as Nayali's gold eyes lingered on my breasts, traveling along the dips of my hips, further down towards that little patch of hair where my pussy was already wet.

"You're beautiful too, Naya." She was stunning, all vivacious curves and smooth skin.

"Do you want to see?" she asked cheekily, and I bit my lip. She stripped off her typical uniform of the band around her breasts and high waisted pants. Naya revealed her teardrop-shaped breasts and her dark nipples. The valleys of her body spoke to me as I drank in her thick waist and thighs. She was bare on her mound, like she had just shaved, and I itched to touch it with my tongue and fingertips.

"You're breathtaking." My belly started to heat as I took her in fully.

"We will play later, princess. First, let's get you bathed and fed." She led me to the bathtub already full of hot water, and I stepped in. She grabbed a washcloth and soap. Gently, Naya started moving along all the planes of my body, teasing my breasts and inner thighs with light touches. I was putty in her hands. She soaped my hair and moved through the tangles until every inch of me had been groomed and my body felt like it was on fire. Every time I reached for her, though, she would tsk and push my hand back down.

"Up, princess," she commanded as I stepped out of the tub into a towel. Nayali dried me off, rubbing me all over. Every touch made me ache for her. She was teasingly me relentlessly with a whisper of something here and there. It was like emotional and physical edging with every touch.

"I laid out an outfit for you, princess. Get dressed, and then we'll eat together and go for a little walk." I nodded as she redressed herself quickly. I watched Nayali, her eyes never leaving mine. The tension in the room was so high, I thought I might combust.

"Naya," I breathed as I watched her walk towards the door.

"No touching yourself, princess. I want you wound up for later." She winked and left me standing there. I grabbed the outfit she laid out, a cropped corset top and a pair of leather leggings with a long, lightweight coat. I slipped everything on quickly and finished it with a pair of boots and two braids in my hair.

Nayali waited outside my door, her eyes dark.

"You look yummy enough to eat." Her fangs poked out a little. "Are you hungry?"

"Starving, actually." The night with Issa had worn me out in an excellent way. I was in desperate need of some fuel. Nayali wrapped me underneath her arm and guided me towards the dining hall, where a romantic table for two waited for us.

We took our seats, and I looked around at the feast in front of us. Every pastry, fruit, meat, and cheese imaginable sat on the table.

"Do you eat food, Naya?" I blurted. I didn't know much about each magical class. My school lessons didn't cover this sort of thing, and I hadn't been much of a student.

"Yes, I do. I need the nourishment of food and of blood. Usually, I get my blood from one of the others. I don't feed directly off them, but rather, we drain it and I drink it throughout the day," Naya said, picking up a piece of bread with jam.

"Why don't you feed directly off them?" I grabbed some fruit and a few pieces of meat.

"It's very intimate. It usually is only meant for your beloved. I fed off Angelica when she was here, and it can be very sexually stimulating for both parties if done correctly. It didn't feel right to do it with anyone else." Naya chewed her food thoughtfully and took a sip of her drink stained deep red.

"Would you...would you feed off me?" I wanted to know what that felt like. I could imagine Nayali sinking her teeth into my neck while her hands stroked a deep, bright fire within me.

"I think I would like to try, princess, if that is what you want as well." Naya reached over and squeezed my hand. "But first, you need to fuel up and hydrate. Then we will talk a bit more about all of that." Naya made me feel so cared for and seen, I could only imagine what that experience would be like.

"Okay, fine. If you say so." I didn't need to be told twice as I dug into everything in front of me and happily filled my belly. I groaned loudly when I couldn't eat another bite.

"Let's get a little fresh air, princess." I nodded as Naya reached for my hand, and we walked out into the sunlight.

"Can you tell me more about vampires? I don't know very much about the nuances and details of magical beings." I nibbled at my thumb, unsure of how to politely ask my questions. "I only know stories, and none firsthand. Most of my life, I have been trying to run away from magic, and here I am, right in the middle of it."

Naya watched me as I spoke. We were walking through a wooded area where the sun fell through the trees in streams, creating a beautiful glow around us.

"I can understand that, princess. It can be hard to embrace things you've been taught to avoid or be afraid of. Vampires have heightened speed and strength similar to fae. We are somewhere between fae and shifters. We have elements of both, sort of animal like but still human. We live much longer than the others as well. We don't possess magic like the fae or energy manipulation, but rather, we can control our own bodies in the human element with less of the animal element.

Our bodies are our biggest asset, and our bloodlust allows us to feel and do more than others."

I nodded. We walked hand in hand through the forest, taking in the surroundings and sharing more stories. I could feel myself falling into the magic that was Naya. She was a steady presence, exuding love, care, and prowess.

We sat in a meadow that looked to be out of a fairy tale. The lighting was soft and angelic, the forest seemed to want to swallow us whole.

"What are you looking for when we fuck, princess?" Nayali didn't mess around, and I nearly choked on air.

"Um...well, I want to know what your tongue piercing feels like." I tried to be brave in saying what I wanted.

"What else, princess?" she asked, tilting her head to the side.

"I want you to drink my blood, and I want you to pull my hair. Just take complete control." I met her eyes, and her gaze seemed to burn into me.

"So you want to try it all, princess?" Her smile widened with each breath I took.

"Yes," I breathed, trying not to squirm under her gaze. My inner thighs started to ache as she licked her lips.

"What safe word did you choose with Issa?"

"Pink."

"It's the same thing, princess. We can stop at any time and re-evaluate or stop. I will bite and feed from you today if you want it, but at any time, you can say the safe word."

I nodded, and my body started to heat. "Should we go?' I said, feeling excited and ready to let Naya take control.

"Let's go, princess. Let's see what your body and mind can handle." And with that, she led me back to the mansion for a night of endless pleasure.

Eight

Nayali led me to her bedroom and shut the door gently behind us. My stomach fluttered with anticipation. The touches she had been giving me throughout the day still lingered on my skin. It was making me edgy and anxious.

"Sit down on the bed, princess," she commanded, and I walked over to her giant bed. Her room was full of warm browns, oranges, yellows, and maroons. It exuded warmth and matched the gold in her eyes.

"Clothes off now, princess." She pulled a chair from the corner of the room and sat down, her forearms on her knees as I began to strip. I slid off my clothes and stood bare in front of her. Nayali's eyes burned into me, her fangs elongating as she took in my nakedness. I could feel the dampness between my thighs, and my nipples hardened under her gaze.

"Do you like this?" I said, straightening my spine, feeling bold. Nayali licked her lips and leaned back in her chair.

"Very much so, princess." My insides seemed to quiver every time she called me that. "Have a seat and spread your legs wide on the edge of the bed." I nodded and laid myself bare in front of her. I knew I was dripping with arousal. I wanted to know what her tongue and fangs felt like.

She stalked over to me and got down on her knees, running her nose along my inner thighs. I moaned as she breathed over my clit and kissed my hip.

"I want you dripping for me when I sink my fangs into you princess." She started to kiss my soft flesh. Her tongue ran up and down my labia, and the cool metal of her tongue ring contrasted the warmth of her mouth.

"I want to know what your piercing feels like," I said as I watched her in awe, worshiping my thighs and hips, getting close to my center but always teasing.

"You mean like this?" She swiped her tongue along my slit, and the cool metal hit the perfect spot. I pressed my breasts high, arching into pleasure.

"Yes," I said as she slid her hands underneath my ass and pulled my pussy to her face to devour me. I whined and moaned as she sucked my clit, swirling the metal to create the most delicious friction that had me riding her face.

"Naya," I cried out as she slipped one, two, three fingers inside me, pumping in and out. She sucked and lapped at my pussy, making me squirm. I held her head between my thighs and groaned into her. The pressure built and had me racing towards my first orgasm. I cried out as my insides quivered, and I fell apart on her mouth.

"What a needy little princess," Nayali said, standing and stripping off her own clothes. I looked hungrily at her as her breasts and mound appeared in front of me. I licked my lips.

"Can I touch you? Please?" I begged. Nayali smiled at me and sat in the chair she had brought over.

"On your knees for me, princess, just like I did for you." She spread her own legs wide, and I scrambled up off the bed to crawl over to her. Her folds were wet and glistening. I leaned in and looked up.

"Like this?" I said, sliding my hands under the globes of her ass and tasting her. God, she tasted divine. She threaded her hand through my hair and pulled gently, guiding my mouth and face as I got lost in her delicious pussy. I could feel another orgasm building inside me as I listened to her moan and groan. The way she used my mouth was absolutely intoxicating.

"That's it, princess. Suck a little harder right there," she commanded. I happily sucked her clit and squeezed her ass as she shuddered around me. "Hazel," she groaned huskily, and I felt her explode around me. I lapped her up as she continued to press my head into her wetness. She grabbed my hair and pulled me up, the pain and pleasure mixing in a delicious convocation.

"Give me that mouth," she said and slammed my lips into hers. I tasted us on her tongue, and it drove me wild. Our lips moved in tandem like it was always meant to be. Her tongue darted in and out, offering the sensation of cool metal against the heat of her lips. I climbed on top of her, grinding into her. I started playing with her tits with my mouth and fingers, pulling softly as she slid her hand down to play with my clit.

"That's it, princess. Keep sucking." I could die in her beautiful breasts as I rode her hand. We both rushed towards another climax as I reached down and circled her clit. She matched my pace and pressed one finger in so we both crashed into our next wave of pleasure, clinging to one another for support.

"Now it's time, princess," she whispered in my ear. She pulled my head to the side, kissing along my neck, her fangs scraping the skin. I shivered, and she guided me off her. Our lips swollen and our fingers wet with another, she released my hair and walked me over to the bed.

"Sit, princess," she commanded, and I plopped down in front of her. Her breasts begged to be touched in front of me.

I licked my lips, looking at her perky nipples. She smiled down at me, exposing the gap in her teeth.

"Can I?" I asked, scooting closer to the end of the bed and looking hungrily at her body.

"Yes, princess. Before we share blood, you can suck on my tits once more." I dove in and worshiped her breasts with my tongue, my hands, my mouth. I could feel my wetness pooling once again on the bed. I desperately wanted to grind into something to release the building pressure as Nayali grabbed my head and pulled away. She twisted my braid around her hand and pulled my head over, exposing my neck.

"Are you ready, princess?" she asked. I nodded, looking up at her and those warm golden eyes that seemed to promise all the pleasure I could ask for. I squirmed as the tension in my center built and Nayali teased me with her teeth. This time, she straddled me, forcing me back on the bed.

Without any warning, her teeth punctured my neck, and I cried out. It was sharp before it melted into the most unbelievable form of ecstasy. My whole body felt warm and lush. It was like a giant orgasm rushed through my entire being and made me shake. Nayali hungrily sucked at it, the sensation pulling at my center, making me explode around her.

We ground into each other, needing all the contact we could get. I reached one hand down to touch myself while Nayali did the same. Wave after wave of pleasure shot through me until we were both groaning into another climax. We collapsed into one another's arms. Nayali looked at me with blood dripping down her chin. I touched a gentle hand to my neck, pulling away to see a few drops of red on my fingers. Nayali grabbed my hand and sucked at my fingertips. It made my whole body erupt in goosebumps.

Ever so delicately, Nayali grabbed a cloth and touched it to the tender spot on my throat.

"That was the most intense thing I have ever felt," I whispered, looking at her.

"In a good way, I hope?" she said, and I nodded with a giggle.

"It was like my whole body was orgasming repeatedly, and every touch sent me over the edge," I said in awe. "Is that how it is for you too?"

"Yes, princess. It feels absolutely addictive," she purred.

"Can we do it again sometime?" I asked, wrapping myself around her as she inhaled.

"Absolutely, princess. You're spectacular, you know that?" she said, burying her face into my neck and licking at the wound, sending electricity through my body with every swipe of her tongue.

"So are you. God, I didn't know how much feeling a tongue piercing could give me, but holy shit." I shivered.

"Oh, there's much more to come, princess," Nayali said. "But now, we rest."

NINE

"God, everyone is getting so much of our delicious Hazel, and I love it." Caro bit into an apple as they leaned against the door frame of Nayali's room. I was starting to realize nothing was hidden between the coven.

"Everything is pretty much out in the open between everyone here?" I asked, sitting up while Nayali buried her face in the pillow.

"Go away, Caro. I want to sleep in more," Nayali mumbled into her pillow.

"You know how I like to rise early, Naya," they said, walking over and scratching her back.

"Yeah, yeah." Her words were swallowed up by the pillow.

"No secrets here, little one. The only way this works is if we are all painfully open and honest, you know? We're all an open book. Do you need some time to yourself?" Caro said, sitting fully on the end of the bed.

"No, I just am not used to having everything out in the open like this, you know?" I chewed my lip and hugged the sheets close to my chest. It was nice to be transparent with everyone. I didn't want any secrets.

"Understandable. Well, little one, we're going to do a little exercise today." Caro smiled devilishly at me.

"Uh..." An image of Caro chasing me through the words and tackling me flashed into my mind. I swallowed thinking of their mouth on mine.

"Ah, little one, some of that will surely happen, but I'm talking about a swim. The day is beautiful and the sun is shining. We can spend some quality time together, and you can ask any questions that might be plaguing that gorgeous mind of yours." Caro got up and finished off their apple.

"Go ahead, Hazel. I'm sleeping for at least a few more hours. You wore me out." Nayali pushed up on her forearms and gazed up at me. I leaned in for a kiss and scooted off the bed, snatching my discarded robe.

Caro watched me carefully as I slipped the black silk fabric on and padded over to where they stood in the doorway.

"Your swimsuit and a coverup are in your room. I will meet you downstairs, alright?" Caro gave my ass a light smack, and I giggled, hustling off to my room to grab what I needed for the day.

I felt like I was in a dream, a sexy and satisfying one where everyone around me truly wanted to care for me. I hadn't had anyone treat me with such reverence and love for a long time. People always wanted something from me, not thinking about what I wanted in return. Instead, this coven had shown me a passion, intensity, and intimacy I hadn't experienced in a long time.

I brushed through my hair quickly and fixed the fly aways. The swimsuit was a one piece, with a low dip in the front and a cheeky bottom. It made me blush slightly as I put it on. It was practically a piece of lingerie. In the mirror, my breasts were nearly half way out, my ass barely contained by the black fabric. I wasn't a small girl. I was thick and soft, and this swimsuit was determined to show all my assets. A sheath dress was placed next to it, so I slipped it on and felt immediately more covered. I wondered what Caro's swimsuit would look like, and the thought made my cheeks blush.

Quickening my pace, I grabbed some sandals and looked for Caro downstairs. I passed Issa on the way, reading a book in a quiet corner of the house. She blew me a kiss.

"Have a good day, love. Caro and you will have the best time!"

I blew a kiss back and smiled as I headed towards the entrance of the house. Caro was lounging in a chair, one leg slung over the slide. Their colorful hair glowed in the sunlight streaming in from the window. They had a smattering of small tattoos across their body that seemed to be hidden and tucked away, only for them to see.

They wore black cargo shorts with laced up boots and a cropped shirt that hung over their muscular core. They were a unique mix of femininity and masculinity. I was eager to know what our bodies could do together.

"Admiring the view, little one?" Caro said, smiling, their tanned skin glowing in the midmorning sun.

"Yes. You're just quite magnificent to look at," I said, embarrassed I had been caught staring.

"You like to lie with all types of people, do you not, little one?" Caro asked, sitting up tall and letting their gaze roam my body. It paused at the bare skin of my thighs and legs.

"I do, yes, but I would say men are not my desired preference most of the time." I had been with people of all shapes, sizes, genders, and sexualities. I liked people for who they were, not for what their physical parts were. I thought all bodies had beauty and desirability, but what made me love and lust for someone was their mind and an emotional connection.

"Good to know, little one. I feel the same. You will see that together, we can make something uniquely ours. I identify with some things in womanhood and some things in manhood, but I identify with neither fully." Caro watched as I listened to them.

"I want to make something that is our own," I replied, walking towards them and standing between their legs.

They ran their hands over the backs of my thighs, and I shivered, my center already wet. Caro inhaled and licked up the front of my leg. I gasped, holding on to their shoulders.

"Yes, little one, we will play with lots of things soon. First, though, we will go have some fun." They stood and placed a gentle kiss to my mouth. I melted against them, my softness folding around the hardness of their chest and arms. "Let's go before I change my mind." They winked and dragged me out the door towards our afternoon adventure.

———

We stood in front of a clear pond, and I looked at it nervously.

"Do you know how to swim, Hazel?" Caro said from next to me. They had shucked off their shirt and wore a compression top around their chest. Their shoulders muscles were on full display, and it made my mouth water. I tried not to look at the sweat sliding down their arms.

"I do. I just am not the best at it," I confessed. I stood in my revealing one piece and grabbed their hand.

"I won't let you drown, little one. I'm a great swimmer. As a shifter, swimming, running, jumping, playing, fighting, fucking...it all comes a little bit more naturally because of my animal side." Caro lifted my fingers to their mouth and dusted a light kiss over my knuckles.

"What can you shift to?" I asked, wanting to run my hands through their colorful stands and scrape my teeth against their bottom lip.

"Most animals are accessible to me, but I prefer large land

creatures. The leopard is my favorite and most practiced. Would you like to see?" They squeezed my hand.

"Yes please!" I said excitedly, turning to face them fully. They stood several inches taller than me, and I had to gaze up to find their eyes.

In a blink of an eye, they shifted into a powerhouse of a cat. I saw their eyes shine through even in animal form, and I reached out to pet their soft fur. They purred in response and nuzzled against me.

"You're extraordinary, Caro," I said, and they shifted back, keeping their nose against my neck.

"Now trust me, little one, and relax in the water." They stood, and we waded into the cool pond together. The bottom wasn't too deep; I could touch it if I stood on my tippy toes. Caro paddled around and splashed me playfully.

I laughed as I splashed back, and it turned into a full out water war. Both of us giggled as Caro grabbed for me, and I hooked my legs around their waist.

"Little one..." Their voice had dropped an octave, and it sent a shiver down my spine. They walked me out with me wrapped around them and laid me down on the shore.

"Caro," I said, aching for their touch. I knew my swimsuit clung to my body with little to nothing not on display.

"I want to devour that ass and your tits," they purred. I arched up towards them, and they slammed their mouth onto mine, covering my body. I groaned as we tore into each other with hands, teeth, and tongue, writhing on the bank of the pond.

"Caro," I moaned, scraping my nails against their spine and wrapping my legs around them once again.

"Time to go, little one. The rest of our exercise awaits." They pulled me up and squeezed me against them. Their hands palmed the globes of my ass. We ran all the way back to the mansion, eager to see what else we could find.

TEN

C aro had many toys already laid out. They had prepared before we even left this morning. There were all sorts of things, like plugs, dildos, clamps, and other objects I was unfamiliar with, plus lots of lubrication.

"I like anal play, little one," Caro said as I looked in awe at the collection on their bed.

"Do you like it for you as well, or do you only like to do it to others?" I asked, touching things gingerly. Caro's room was clean and vibrant. Colors were splashed around, and everything seemed to be unique. Still, it all had a cohesive feel. It never should have gone together, but somehow, it did, in an aesthetic that seemed all their own.

"I like it both ways, but my preference is to use this and fuck you in the ass." They reached for a leather harness with a dildo attached to it. It seemed like a belt of sorts. I had only ever done a little anal play, but I did like it.

"What is it exactly?" I looked at it, wondering how it would work.

"I put it around my waist and hips so I have access to that tight little hole of yours." Caro smiled at me, licking their lips.

"Okay...can we go slow?" I was suddenly feeling very nervous. I didn't want to disappoint Caro, but I was scared. I couldn't imagine how something that large would fit in such a tiny hole.

"Of course, little one. I will get you nice and ready before we graduate to that. Would you like to start playing?" Caro's claws were out, and they stroked them against my arm, almost tickling.

"Yes." I nodded, and they moved the toys so there was enough room for us on the large bed.

"Let's start with no clothes. Why don't you undress both of us, little one?" Caro said, and I nodded, removing my things first. Caro's eyes roamed across my breasts and hips.

"Turn around and bend over, little one," Caro commanded, and I did as I was told. I bent over the bed, my nipples hardening now that they were exposed.

"Spread your cheeks for me," Caro hummed, and I reached behind me, pulling my ass apart, exposing the most sensitive and hidden spot.

"Beautiful, little one. That ass is mine," Caro growled. They grabbed my hands and pulled me up, spinning me around.

"Can I undress you now?" I asked, and they nodded. I carefully slipped off their clothes, my hands roaming across their chest. Their own nipples were hard; they were a mix of hard and soft all over their body. I stripped off the last piece of clothing and found the curly brown tuft of hair at the apex of their thighs.

"You are mesmerizing," I said, running my hands along the small bumps of their chest and down their muscular arms.

"As are you, little one," Caro said, stepping into me. I wrapped my arms around them, and they hoisted my legs up so I could hook my ankles around their waist. Our mouths clashed hungrily as we tasted each other. They bit and nipped at my lips, and I moaned into them.

I could feel Caro's claws biting into my ass. They started to nip and suck down the length of my neck as we backed up onto the bed, where they threw me forcefully down. Suddenly, Caro's hands, teeth, and lips were everywhere at once, sucking and teasing every part of me. Just as I felt the wave of pleasure rising within me, they would move to the next erogenous spot. My neck. Inner thighs. Everywhere.

"Give me that pussy, Hazel," Caro growled and pulled my legs forward before they flipped me. I yelped, not expecting to be on my stomach as they ate me out from behind. Their tongue dove into me with vigor, like they were starving and I was the only thing left to eat on this Earth. Their tongue and fingertips darted around my clit and in and out of my wet folds. They ventured their tongue around my puckered hole, and the sensation surprised me. It was equal parts pleasurable and new. I felt something deeper within me rise to meet this new feeling.

My pussy quivered as their tongue and their finger, wet and cold with lube, dived into my ass. I found myself grinding against them as their other fingers played with my clit. My first orgasm roared within me as all the places inside me were filled with Caro's deft fingers and tongue. I shuddered around them, gripping the sheet as the first wave of pleasure crashed into me.

"Ah, so my little Hazel does know how to come with that beautiful ass of hers," Caro praised. They reached for something, and I felt coolness against my puckered hole.

"This is a plug, little one. I am putting it in so you can get a taste of me. You aren't allowed to take it out until I say. Do you understand?" Caro asked, sliding the coolness inside me. I felt myself stretch, shuddering as the plug settled into me. I felt full in a new way.

"Yes, Caro," I groaned, my face still down against the bed.

"And this also stays in, do you understand?" Caro said, sliding what felt like two balls into my pussy. Suddenly, I was even more full.

"Yes, Caro," I repeated. They pulled me up, and the friction in my body was immediate. My insides quivered as the balls shifted and the plug settled in. I gasped and wiggled around.

"Do you like that?" Caro said, looking hungrily at me.

"It feels so good," I mumbled, reveling in the new sensation.

"Get on all fours, little one," Caro commanded as they sat at the edge of the bed. I nodded obediently and sank down, each movement creating more friction inside me.

"I want you to eat me out the way I did, front to back. Do you understand? Use your fingers and tongue." I nodded as they spread themselves wide, and I crawled to them. They laid down, and I positioned myself in front of their wetness. God, they smelled good. I dove in, wanting to lose myself in Caro's sense of adventure. With every swipe of my finger and tongue, I grew bolder as I made my way towards Caro's ass. I wasn't used to doing this, but I wanted to touch and taste the most intimate parts of Caro like they did me.

I grew bolder and licked around their puckered hole.

"Yes, little one. You can do more," they encouraged.

I gently worked one finger in, and the pressure was intense on my finger.

"Another one, little one. You can give me more," Caro commanded.

I put another one in and marveled at the sounds and movements Caro made. It made my own wetness pool around the balls. Caro raced towards their orgasm as they commanded me where to put more and less pressure, where to place fingers and my tongue. It was like a beautifully orchestrated dance as they conducted me in their own satisfaction.

They finally cried out, grabbing my head and pressing my face into their most sensitive area. Panting, they rolled up and licked their lips, their claws on full display and their eyes glowing.

"On all fours, ass up on the bed, little one. It's time." I scrambled on the bed as they stepped off, strapping themselves into the leather harness with the large dildo at the end. They squirted lubrication on it, and my eyes widened. I looked forward and felt Caro take out the plug, keeping the balls inside me.

I felt the coolness of the lube press against my hole, and Caro commanded me to breathe as they started to sheath themselves, inch by glorious inch, until they were settled against my ass.

"I'll take it slow, little one," Caro said, and they started to thrust gently and deeply into me. My body quivered with each delicious stroke. Caro reached around and played with my clit at the same time. So many sensations of fullness and pleasure raced through me. I felt my body explode around them as I yelled out and the orgasm ripped through me. They continued to move inside me as my orgasm made its way from my head to my toes.

"That's it, little one. Do you like when I'm in your ass?" Caro asked, gripping me hard and massaging my buttocks. I hadn't noticed their claws against my flesh, but the slight stinging told me there would be marks there. Oddly, that made me happy.

"Yes, Caro," I said, shivering around them. They slowly slid out and flipped me over again.

"I'm coming on top of you again, little one." I nodded as

they discarded their harness and placed themselves on top of my face.

"Eat me," they commanded, and I ravaged them again. I couldn't think of anywhere else I would rather be. I would be happy to drown in the essence of Caro. We both raced towards climaxes as I fingered their asshole while tongue fucking them. Their hands played with my aching nub.

We cried out at the same time and collapsed, fully spent. Caro recovered faster and pulled me on top of them, ravishing my lips once more, our scents and wetness mingling in something deliciously our own.

"You're feral, little one. I like it," Caro purred.

"That was the best ass fucking I've ever received," I said stroking their nipples. I revealed at how they shivered when I touched their chest.

"It will only get better, little one. And bigger." I gasped, not believing anything bigger could fit back there.

"But for now, close your eyes and rest. You've had quite a few days." Their claws stroked me as they recounted their favorite childhood memories and how they would run feral through the woods until sleep took me as I sprawled in Caro's arms.

ELEVEN

I woke up to the feeling of being watched. Scarlett stood in the corner, silently looking at me and Caro without a word. In fact, she actively looked displeased. I didn't know if I had done something wrong or not. The others seemed totally fine that we were all together, so I imagined it was just my existence that irritated Scarlett.

Caro roused next to me and pulled me close. They opened their eyes, and this time, Scarlett did smile.

"It's creepy that you're just standing there scowling, Scar," Caro said, barely lifting their lids.

"Well, I didn't want to wake you all prematurely. I know how much you like your beauty rest," Scar teased, and Caro threw a pillow at her haphazardly. Scar laughed, a magical sound.

"Take your time getting dressed, Hazel. I will be in the garden waiting for you with food on the table," Scar stated and then swept out of the room.

"I don't think she likes me." I sighed, snuggling deeper into Caro's bare chest.

"Oh, I think she does. I think that's why she is so scowly and grumpy." Caro chuckled.

"Really?"

"Yes, little one. She just needs time. Best not keep her waiting. Go along and get ready for your day with her." I stood, and Caro slapped my ass loudly. The slap stung slightly, only to be soothed by their fingers. I yelped and then moaned at Caro's playful hands.

"Oooh, you like that, little one?" Caro asked smugly. "Nex time." They pulled me in close, kissing me loudly, ravishing my mouth.

"You're going to make her wait longer!" I squealed, running from them as they grinned lazily.

"So much more pleasure in store for you, little one. I'll see you soon." They collapsed back on the bed, and I headed to my own rooms. I ran into Nayali on the way, and she licked the column of my neck, sending me into a fit of giggles and arousal.

Issa caught me as well, sliding her hand around my breasts and tweaking my nipples. I smiled as I tore myself away from each of them.

All of them showed their adoration and care for me except Scarlett. I got nervous once more as I quickly dressed and headed out to the garden. She sat quietly, her red hair flaming in the sunlight, her green eyes piercing into me.

"Hi, Scarlett," I said, feeling very self-conscious sitting across from her. Her generous breasts were barely contained, and her honey colored legs were bare, soaking up the sun.

"Are you enjoying your time with us, Hazel?" she said, giving nothing away in her tone or her expression.

"Yes, I love it here. I love…" I almost said I love all of them, but I quickly decided against it. It was too fast, too soon. "I love this place and the relationships I'm building with you all."

Scarlett smiled then. "I know my demeanor seems harsher than the others. Angelica felt like my one true beloved. I'm hoping we can fuel the spark between us, Hazel," she said, grabbing for her tea as I grabbed a piece of meat.

"You feel a spark between us?" I asked, slightly shocked. I didn't know Scarlett felt anything for me.

"Oh, yes. Caro was correct in saying it's why I'm so taciturn." Scarlett stood, and I sat still as she positioned herself behind me, running her hands down my body.

I moaned as her palms grabbed my breasts and her fingertips traveled along my body through my clothes. She plunged her fingers into my panties, and I was already wet for her to play with.

"See, I know you know there's something here, darling. Your pussy is practically begging for me to fuck it," she purred in my ear. She pulled my head back, and my pussy suddenly felt empty without her fingers in it.

She pulled out one of her breasts. They were big and beautiful, her nipples a soft rose pink.

"Suck my tits, Hazel," she demanded, shoving my mouth onto her. I didn't complain as she pushed her breasts in my face to lick and taste. She groaned as I moved between each one. She pushed my head back up so I was facing forward and she was still standing behind me.

Scarlett's hands slid down in front of me again, making their way to my aching core. I moaned as she quickly drew pleasure from me.

"You don't get to come until I say, darling. We have much more to do and play with today." I raced towards the edge and fought to keep control of my pleasure as her fingers circled my center. Quickly, Scar left me panting and wet, right at the edge of orgasm.

She walked back around to her seat and sucked her fingers.

"You are quite an exquisite flavor, Hazel," she said, her eyes on fire now. "Eat up, and we'll talk more." I felt like I had whiplash from the casualness of her tone and the intensity of what just happened in my panties.

I nodded, eating everything I could. The past few days had been amazing but exhausting, so I ate up everything with rigor. Scar was so hot and cold. I didn't want to upset her, but I didn't know what she wanted from me.

Once I had eaten everything in sight, she stood, offering her hand.

"Let's go play dress up," she said and pulled me into the house. I wondered what that meant, but I was excited to find out. She led me up several flights of stairs into an expansive open room with racks of lingerie and coordinating outfits.

"You will put on a little fashion show for me, darling, and I will watch." She started to fling her clothes off, her voluptuous body on full display. Her large breasts seemed to stay perfectly in place, and her creamy skin had hardly any blemishes at all. She sat in what looked like a throne and threw her legs wide. She grabbed a toy from the side, pressed a button, and it whirred to life. I watched as she placed it inside her and moved on it in a delicious fashion. I was mesmerized by her fucking herself, and I started to involuntarily reach my hand down towards my own pussy.

She tsked and shook her head." No, darling, you get to play dress up, and I will watch as I fuck myself. Then, you will get your turn." I was salivating as I squeezed my thighs together. Everything inside me was begging to be released . She commanded me to try on nearly everything in the room. I would try on scraps of lace, and she would demand I walk around and bend over or touch myself in small ways, all while she continued to watch and play with herself.

It was excruciating not being able to do anything about it. We continued the game with flowy silk pieces and thigh harnesses. Some showed off my curves and breasts while others floated in the warm air. My skin and pussy were practically on fire. I would toss the item I just wore to her, and she would smell where my cunt had been before she licked it.

I was being driven wild, and she didn't even need to touch me. This woman was the most powerful person I had ever reckoned with. We continued this song and dance until it was dark. Scarlett had moaned and worked herself several times over.

Finally, she smiled and put her toys down.

"It's time, Hazel. Do you feel worked up?" she asked smoothly. I was ready to combust. I nodded. We hardly spoke the whole day, but I felt like she saw and knew every detail about me from how she commanded my body.

"Then let's get to it," she said, and I shuddered.

She plunged her hand into my pussy, and that touch alone sent me into my first orgasm.

"One, darling," Scarlett whispered as I exploded around her with just a little touch.

"Let's see how many we can get you to tonight." She slipped it out and stuck her fingers back into her own pussy before she grabbed a glass of water for me.

"Drink up. You'll need to stay hydrated for what I have in store."

And boy, did I need it. The night had only just begun.

TWELVE

"Lie down, darling," Scarlett said. We were in another room with many toys and things I was unfamiliar with.

I was guided to a chaise lounge, handcuffs strapped around each leg. I could lay down just enough for my head to be at the top and my knees to hit the bottom. Scarlett hooked me in. She smiled sinisterly as her nails scraped against my ankles and wrists.

"Comfortable, darling?" she inquired, and I nodded, my mouth dry but my pussy wet. I was naked and laid out in front of her. I didn't know what to expect at this point. She walked over to a table and picked something up. She waved her hands over it, and it started vibrating. My eyes went wide.

"For every orgasm you give me, you must drink one glass of water and you can ask me one question. Do you understand, Hazel?" she asked seriously. We had barely talked all day. It was more like she commanded me, and I listened during our fashion show.

I nodded and watched her sultry body move over to me. My legs were already spread wide because of the cuffs. She looked hungrily down at my pussy. Scarlett put the phallic-shaped toy in her mouth and licked the whole thing. I watched her deep throat it and pull it out.

"This is going in your pussy. Would you like that?" It dripped with her saliva, and I could feel heat rushing to the apex of my thighs.

She reached down and slid one finger along the length of my folds. I groaned and shuddered. She took it away, and it glistened with my arousal. She popped it into her mouth, and my whole body tingled as I watched her.

"I would like that," I whispered. My body was wound so tight. That one orgasm had barely done anything to the tension she had been building all day.

"I thought so. I'm going to put this in you, and it will vibrate. I'm going to change. You aren't allowed to come until I get back alright?"

I nodded.

"Answer out loud, Hazel. Say yes, madam." Her tone sent shivers down my spine.

"Yes, madam."

She smiled again at me like I had done something good, and it pleased me greatly.

"Good girl. Your safe word is still the same. Use the word pink if anything makes you uncomfortable or doesn't feel good. Do you understand?" The toy was still vibrating in her hand.

"Yes, madam."

"Good, I want you to lick this too, and then we'll put it in your wet little cunt." She walked over to where my head was, and I opened my mouth wide to receive the toy. It was wet with Scarlett's own saliva, but the thought of our spit mixing and then going inside me created a new kind of warmth.

She pulled it out with a pop and moved to where I was

soaking the chaise lounge with my desire. She parted my pussy lips, and I groaned as she pressed the tip to my.

"No orgasm yet. I need to put my outfit on," Scarlett purred. She wore just a robe at the moment, and I could catch glimpses of her silky skin. She slid the dildo in, and it stretched and filled me in a delicious way. It vibrated against my inner-most walls. She gave it a few pumps, and I had to fight the orgasm that threatened to rip through me. I wanted to please Scarlett, so I wiggled and groaned.

"Good girl. I can see you trying to fight it. I will leave it in and take it out when I come back." She pushed it to the hilt and left, swaying her hips. Fuck, the vibration felt good, but I couldn't get the exact friction I needed. It was such a tease to be filled but not get what you want.

I breathed deeply, wanting to touch my clit or grab my nipples, but I couldn't do any of those things. I closed my eyes and waited until she came back. I had no idea how long it took, but she finally strutted back into the room, her heels clacking. She stood over me in a shiny latex outfit that shoved her generous tits up and left little to the imagination. Her ass was plump and her thighs rubbed together. Every part of her was luscious, and I wanted to touch it all.

"Good girl. No orgasms yet." She leaned down and kissed me deeply. I arched into her, and she reached for the toy.

"Now you can orgasm," she whispered against my mouth, pumping the toy in and out of me as her lips met mine in soft and slow kisses. I groaned as my orgasm raced to meet her. It took less than five seconds, and I exploded, pulsating and throbbing from the edging.

"Madam!" I cried out.

"Sounds so sweet on your lips." Scarlett started to unshackle me, and I was putty in her arms. She took me over to another piece of furniture, where I was commanded to lay down on my belly with my face down and ass up.

"Caro prepared your ass well," she purred from behind me. Suddenly, something was pushing at my back entrance, and it felt full and sweet, just as my pussy had moments ago. The vibrations started again, and I groaned as it reached a deep spot inside me I didn't know needed stroking.

Scarlett pulled my hips so my pussy was on full display and accessible to her mouth. She dove in, lapping and sucking at my clit while the vibration continued in my ass. I groaned as I ground into her face and grabbed my nipples, pulling hard.

"Don't come until I say so, darling," Scarlett reminded me. I stopped pulling at my tits and focused on the building pleasure, not letting it crest as Scarlett tongue fucked me for what felt like hours.

"Now you can come," she said, sucking on my clit. She stood and started moving the toy in and out of my ass. It created a deep warmth in me, a wave just begging to crest. I let it go as the second orgasm from anal slammed into my body. I cried out and my legs shook. She milked each wave as she pumped the toy in and out.

"That's it, darling." She slipped it out and cleaned me up before she lifted me again and handed me a glass of water.

"Drink. You will get another for the two orgasms." I could barely stand as I slammed down the water, and she waved her hand, filling it again.

"You have two questions you can ask when we are done here, darling," Scarlett said and walked me over to the large bed in the middle of the room.

"Now, those pretty titties of yours." She wrapped a blindfold around my eyes. I felt her all around me. I wanted to please her so badly. She played with my nipples, pinching and pulling, sucking and licking with those full lips. I felt her wet heat on me as she straddled and dove in. I could feel another orgasm start to pull at my core with just my titties being played with.

"Come hard for me, darling," Scarlett commanded, and it came on so hard and fast. I shuddered as everything around me exploded, made so much more intense by my eyes being covered. I barely had time to recover as she opened my legs wide and tongue fucked me again.

"Come again."

My body was hers to command. I writhed and wriggled for her as I felt another taking me by surprise.

She had complete control of me as she moved me into different positions, used different toys, and commanded my orgasm to come again and again. Water. Orgasm. Repeat. We reached twelve orgasms, and my body felt raw. I couldn't give another, and I told her that.

"You did good, darling. Twelve is a lot. Twelve questions are yours." I was pleased with the compliment as I lay spent on the bed, sweat on my skin, my breath uneven.

"When will I get to make you come?" I said. The whole session had been her giving to me, and I didn't get to reciprocate.

"You have to earn it, darling, but you're well on your way." She smiled lovingly at me and stroked my hair. "I'll be back." She walked out the door, her ass jiggling as she strutted away.

I thought I had done a good job. I was excited to please her too when she allowed it. I could barely keep my eyes open though and drifted off to sleep before she returned.

THIRTEEN

My dreams were even filled with pleasure. I dreamt of all of them fucking my face and then me doing the same to them, Caro in my ass and Naya grinding down on me, Scarlett tying me up and Issa branding me. I dreamed of two of them using me and then three and then all four of them. I wanted to be their one and only. I groaned as the dreams slipped away from me, and I woke in the bed Scarlett had used me in.

Food was set next to me, and I dove at it like I was starved. I wondered where Scarlett was. I was a little disappointed she hadn't slept in here. It seemed like her boundaries were still high with me, her protective walls firmly in place from what had happened with Angelica.

The door cracked open, and Issa walked in. She smiled broadly at me, and I hopped up, scattering the food as I ran to her. Our bodies collided, and she laughed.

"Did you miss me, love?" she said, combing my hair as I nuzzled her neck.

"Yes. I'm also feeling a bit self-conscious." The words tumbled out as she led me back over to the bed and handed me another piece of bread I tore into. She carefully picked up the scattered food and handed me some water.

"Why don't you tell me about it?" she soothed. There was something about Issa that always made me feel loved.

"Scarlett," I blushed, trying to think of how to say it.

"You don't need to be embarrassed about anything that happens in this house, love. We're all very aware." She gave my knee a little squeeze.

"Well, she gave me so many orgasms, but we barely talked, and she wouldn't allow me to do the same to her. I did win twelve questions because that's how many times I came, but I don't know if I did well." I nibbled nervously on some food.

"I promise you, love, you did well. She would tell you if you didn't. Scarlett is just a tough emotional nut to crack. It will take time. I know she likes you; she just has to let you in." She stroked my arm, and I melted into her.

"We played with so many toys I didn't know existed." I giggled thinking of all the ways my body had responded. I had no idea there were so many orgasms just waiting to be pulled out of me.

Issa chuckled. "Scarlett truly has magical powers. She can make someone explode in pleasure. It's miraculous." Issa stood and held her hand out.

"What's going on today?" I asked, standing. I was still naked but I was getting more comfortable with my body on full display around them.

"We're going to go out on a group outing! Now that you have had time with each of us alone, we thought it might be fun to go out together. Scarlett sent me to retrieve you, as she had some business this morning." Issa wove our fingers together and pulled me out of the sex room.

My skin tingled from our connection as we walked hand in hand back to my room.

"Do you want help getting ready, or do you want some

time alone?" Issa asked as we stood in my room. I bit my lip. I thought I would be more than satiated from last night, but I hadn't tasted Issa in a couple of days, and her body seemed to call to me.

"Issa..." I whispered, looking at her. She slowly shut the door behind us with a smile on her face, as if she already knew what I needed.

"I know that look, love." She stalked over to me.

"Can I taste you please?" I begged, and she slipped off her clothes, her tattoos beautiful against her pale skin. We collided, with hands and tongues grabbing and squeezing everything we could get a hold of. Her mouth tasted right against mine, and we both slipped fingers into one another, groaning simultaneously. It was a dance our bodies seem to have memorized already.

We pulled away, and I scrambled up on the bed, lying down so Issa could sit on my face. She grabbed the headboard and started to fuck my face as I devoured her wetness and worshipped her pretty pussy. I slid my tongue in and worked my finger against her engorged clit.

"Yes, love. Right there," she said, grinding herself against the flat part of my tongue. She came around me, moaning my name while continuing to ride my face. The door burst open to my room suddenly, and Nayali stood there, her eyes blazing.

"I want a ride too."

Issa got off me, and Nayali stripped as she climbed on top and shoved her pussy lips over my mouth. Nayali groaned as I grabbed the globes of her ass and got lost in the scent and feeling of her.

"Wow, Nayali, you look good riding Hazel," Issa mused. She placed herself in between my thighs and started lapping at my pussy. I squirmed underneath Nayali, but she held me in place, riding me while Issa ate me out. It was so sensual and delicious, I slammed into my orgasm at full speed. Nayali crashed into hers, and we were all panting and sweaty together. The smell of sex hung heavy in the air. I could get drunk off it.

"What a fun thing to walk into," Caro said, leaning against the door.

"Do you want a turn on Hazel's pretty face?" Nayali asked, climbing off. My body tingled with the thought of all of us together.

"Since you offered." Caro stripped off their clothes and climbed on top of me. "Can you go another round, little one?" I nodded eagerly, and they sat on my lips. I could have died from pleasure.

"My turn to eat this tight little pussy," Nayali said, diving into my arousal that was already so sensitive from Issa's tongue.

"It gives me time with these beautiful tits," Issa said.

The sensations were overwhelming with Caro on top of me. I clung to them like they were the only thing keeping me grounded. Issa played with my titties and sucked my aching nipples. Nayali devoured my cunt. Pleasure came at me from all directions, and I thought I would combust until Caro started to shake.

Issa and Nayali also started to moan. I assumed they played with their pussies while they worked magic with their mouths. It was a symphony of ecstasy as we all raced to our climax.

We collapsed on the bed, a tangle of arms, legs and hair.

"That was delicious to watch," Scarlett said from the corner. I gasped, not even realizing she was there, her wet hand slipping out of her panties as she stalked over and shoved her fingers in my mouth.

"You'll taste it soon, darling, but this is just a tease." I lapped it up as Issa chuckled and Caro sighed. Nayali nuzzled next to me.

"We all need to get ready. I know Hazel has the power to keep us all connected to our beds, but we do have other things to accomplish," Scarlett teased, and slowly, we all untangled ourselves. Each one planted a kiss on my mouth and caressed me in some way. My ass, my tits, my jaw, each one special and different from the last.

"See you in an hour, love," Issa said.

"Shower up, little one." Caro waved.

"Drink your water, princess," Nayali commanded.

"Behave, darling," Scarlett said. She was the last one out the door.

I collapsed on my bed, not believing I could be here with these wonderful beings. I smiled and hugged myself, excited for what was to come. I started to get ready for a day I was sure to never forget.

FOURTEEN

They all waited for me downstairs at the entrance of the house. The four of them together was a formidable wall, all so different but absolutely extraordinary. I knew little about their powers besides what they had shared, so I hoped I would see more as time went on.

"What are we doing today?" I asked as I stepped up to them. Issa reached for my one hand, Nayali the other.

"We're heading into the market today, little one. It should be bustling with energy and delicious food and lots of things to catch your eye," Caro said, caressing my jaw. Scarlett opened the door and ushered us out.

"I can't wait to show you my favorite vendor, who has the most incredible sweets," Issa said. Her hand was warm and comfortable in my own.

"Don't forget about that little bookstore we all like!" Nayali chimed in.

"And the pleasure shop," Scarlett purred, looking at me wickedly. I blushed under her gaze, but I was excited to see what lay beyond the mansion walls. Caro shifted into their leopard form and ran wild, roaring and whipping past us. We laughed and giggled as they slinked between our legs and nuzzled up against us.

The sun was high today, and a cool breeze seemed to tickle my skin. It was the perfect day to explore. Chatter flowed effortlessly between the five of us, and we truly felt like a family. A warmth grew in my chest that made me practically glow. I hadn't felt safe and loved for a very long time.

Soon, we happened upon the village market, and it was a plethora of sounds, sights, and smells. Issa dragged me over to the sweets shop first, where we got chocolate and taffy. We giggled as we fed each other little samplings of each and then licked the remains off the other's fingertips. Quickly and quietly, Issa pulled me into an alleyway and ravished my mouth, the scent of sugar on both of our lips and tongues.

"Come on, you two! Plenty of time for that later," Naya said, dragging us with her, and we burst into giggles.

Everyone crowded into a bookstore, and we each dispersed to our favorite genres and styles. Nayali caught me in the romance section tucked into a corner.

"I just love the smell of books," she said dreamily, running her fingertips along the spines.

"Me too. Romance has always been my favorite," I said, looking wistfully at the tall shelves. Nayali came up behind me and wrapped her arms around my waist. Her breath was hot on my neck.

"You are quite the insatiable little sex kitten, so I can see why these might appeal to you," Nayali said, nibbling at my ear. Her fangs popped out, and she slid them along the length of my neck. My pussy instantly became wet as I revisited the memory of Nayali feeding from me.

"Naya," I breathed as her hands traveled to my breasts and pulled at my nipples. I arched into her, her fangs pushing deeper into my skin.

"Not here, princess, but at home. I will need to feed." She

gave my nipples one last tweak and left me breathless in the romance section. I aimlessly grabbed a few books and joined the others blushing and wet. They all looked hungrily at me, as if they could smell my arousal. We departed the book store and pressed back into the crowd of the market.

Scarlett wrapped her arm around me and guided me through the maze of shops and vendors to a special shop with a doorbell. She rang it and was immediately let in. The shop was dark and sensual, with many toys on display.

"Pick something you like, darling. We will play later," she said. Scarlett moved to a couple of different displays and chatted with the shop owner like they were good friends. I grabbed a few different things I thought looked interesting, and the owner smiled kindly as they bagged it up. Instead of going out the way we came, we headed to a different door to a hallway that branched off into several other rooms.

Scarlett seemed to know where she was going as she opened the door, the others already waiting inside. They all lounged on a large sofa, a bed in the middle.

"What is this room?" I asked, not understanding.

"A private room you rent by the hour, darling. We're all hungry for you, so I thought we would make a little pit stop before we got home," Scarlett said, hanging the bag of our purchases up on a hook.

My pussy immediately responded, thinking about what we could all do together in this room, of all of them wanting me now and not being able to wait until we got home.

"Do you like the idea of that, little one?" Caro and grabbed my chin, diving in with their tongue. I was putty in their hands as they shredded my clothes with their claws. All the fabric floated to the ground, leaving me naked in front of them.

"How about...Caro in your ass, me in your pussy, and the others on your breasts? Maybe we take turns?" Issa hummed.

"I would like that," I mumbled as Caro fiddled in a drawer, pulling a harness and dildo on. Grabbing lubrication, Caro commanded me to bend over the bed and spread my cheeks as they slowly started to work their fingers in, then the dildo. When I could take the whole thing, Caro led me over to the sofa, where I slid onto the dildo, my back against Caro's strong chest. I groaned as it pierced through me and touched all my most sensitive parts. Caro spread my legs wide, my thighs on the outside of theirs.

"Issa, come taste our dirty girl," Caro growled, playing with my tits and biting my neck. Issa sauntered over and kneeled in front of me. I was splayed open, raw and ready to be devoured. My wetness dripped onto the floor. Issa wasted no time as she dove, sucking and lapping at my clit.

Naya and Scarlett hungrily descended as they each took one of my breasts. They all moved inside and around me, creating a cornucopia of sensation. I lost track of how many orgasms I had as they raced through my body again and again. I groaned as they each took turns feasting on my pussy and sucking my clit, my breasts, and fucking my asshole.

I felt used in the most delicious way. I wanted to stay like this forever. I would be their magic life blood. I would give anything to hand my body over to them.

"Now you eat from us, little one." Caro growled and shoved my face down, where I gave as much as I took. They each tasted different, unique, and I loved giving them as much as I loved receiving.

Scarlett was last, and I kneeled in front of her tentatively.

"You earned it, darling. You can feast on me." She stroked my hair and cheek lovingly. I took my time licking and sucking every part of her pussy and her breasts as she groaned and dominated me.

It was a beautiful combination of sex and connection, everything out in the open, pleasure the pinnacle of it all.

When I made Scarlett orgasm, I felt like I was on top of the world. We all collapsed into a pile of limbs. I was snuggled in between Scarlett and Naya. I wondered how long we could stay here. If I could, I would never leave.

FIFTEEN

We cleaned up quickly and headed out of the pleasure house to grab some lunch. The feeling was light and magical. I had been thinking about the twelve questions I wanted to ask Scarlett. We still hadn't gotten a chance to really talk, and I wanted to make my questions count.

Our group rounded the corner towards Caro's favorite lunch spot when we came face to face with Saul.

"Oh, look at that. The mortal has settled in with your band of filth," he spat at us. The other three men in his coven loitered behind him. They all looked the same: broad and brutish with rough edges.

"You know better than to speak to us." Nayali stepped in front of me and shoved her nose in Saul's face. He was forced to take a step back.

"You won't do anything out here, Nayali. People will talk if a skirmish occurs." He pushed his chest into her. She didn't budge.

"So what's the reason for this display of toxic masculinity then, hmm?" Scarlett asked, her tone razor sharp.

Saul looked her up and down, his eyes hungry. "Are you sure you don't want to trade some of your coven for mine?"

Issa scoffed. "None of us are interested in what you can offer, Saul. I don't know what makes you think any of us would want what you're offering after what you did with Angelica."

Saul shrugged like it wasn't a big deal, and I felt rage boil up inside me. "How dare you act like what you did wasn't some heinous act?" I growled, lunging for him, but Caro held me back.

"Oh, the little mortal has a feisty side." His eyes lit up at my fight.

"You will never touch Hazel," Caro growled.

"What exactly do you want, Saul? What will it take for you to leave us the fuck alone?" Scarlett said, crossing her arms and staring him down.

"I want her back. She was ours first. We found her, and Nayali here stole her away."

"She is not a piece of property. Hazel wanted to leave, and you were holding her captive," Naya hissed at him.

"Why do you think you are above the law, Saul? A coven is supposed to be about love and support, not selfishness, manipulation, and violence," Issa seethed.

"No one knows if that really matters. What matters is that there are five and the ritual is complete. The other nuances and rules are unimportant in the struggle for power," Saul sneered, like he was above the rules.

"Your disregard for the traditions of the practice shows, you piece of shit. That is why your coven is weak! That is why you must resort to violence to get a mortal woman." Caro's claws popped out like they were ready to tear Saul's face apart.

"Then why was it so easy to take your Angelica, hm?" Saul taunted. I felt the moment the tension broke around us. Scarlett roared as she slammed her hands out, sending energy shooting through them right at Saul's chest. He fell back and hit the ground with a thud. The rest of his men hollered and charged at us.

Soon, it was a full out brawl in the middle of the market. Magic sizzled in the air as Caro went full shifter mode. Claws and teeth flashed as blood sprayed and whimpers echoed around us.

Nayali found her match in the other vampire, and they moved at hyper speed with quick punches and kicks. Fangs tore at skin, and blood splattered the ground amidst the violence.

Issa and their fae member rolled and grunted as energy flew around us. The air was crisp and electric as they battled it out with fists and magic. Everything moved so fast, it was hard to understand what was happening.

Saul recovered quickly, and Scarlett went head to head with him in a vicious spell exchange. Sweat pooled on her brow, but anger rolled off her in waves.

Everyone around me was fighting to the death.

I didn't know what to do. I backed away helplessly. Each of their members would take lunges at me periodically, only to be pulled back aggressively by our coven. It was an all-out brawl for what felt like the most power.

The people around us screamed, and chaos ensued.

"Get back to the house, Hazel!" Scarlett screamed, and I looked around at my family.

"Go Hazel," Issa said between exchanges of fists.

"Run, little one," Caro pleaded.

"We will find you!!" Nayali added.

So, I ran. I turned and fled the market, running back the way we came. Tears poured down my cheeks as I hustled away from the battle and did my best not to look back. My legs burned, but I kept going through the forest and the meadows. I could see the faint outline of our house, and I wasn't going to stop until I was at the door.

It felt like someone was chasing me the whole way there, but I didn't dare look back. I pumped my legs and arms as fast I could, only stopping when I felt like I couldn't take one more step. The sun was low in the sky, and I had no idea how long we had been away or what shape my family would be in when they got back to me.

Would Saul and his men kill them? The thought made me want to throw up.

I finally made it to the large doors and threw them open, stumbling inside. Latching the wooden bolt across the door just like they had shown me, I fled to my room. Exhaustion overtook me, and I collapsed on my bed. Tears started to fall, and my whole body shook.

I was so angry. How could Saul just attack my loved ones like that? Why couldn't he just leave us alone? Eventually, the angry tears stopped, and I waited for what felt like hours.

Finally, I showered and scrubbed the day off my body. I thought about how, just this morning, we were all enjoying the pleasures of each other, and then Saul fucked it up. I wanted to rip his eyeballs out and tell every single one of the men in his coven to go fuck themselves.

After I scrubbed my skin, the sun had fully set, the moon working its way up in the sky. My anxiety and worry had skyrocketed. What if something happened to one of them? What if they were severely injured or on the brink of death— or worse?

I knew if I stayed, I would have just been in the way. Still, I couldn't help but feel like I should have protected them, just like they were always protecting me.

Sleep pulled at me, and I could hardly keep my eyes open.

I was listening intently for the sound of my family coming home, but it never came. Drowsiness wrapped around me, and I let it take me, hoping when I woke up, I would see the ones I cared for deeply again.

Sixteen

I woke up abruptly. My sheets were tangled around me, and the bed felt empty and cold. I looked around, realizing I never knew if anyone came home last night. Throwing the covers off, I sprinted out of my room. I heard voices downstairs and took the stairs two at a time. My heart was beating wildly. Surely, I would know if something happened to one of them, wouldn't I?

Stumbling, I nearly fell into the dining room, where Issa, Nayali, Caro, and Scarlett sat around the table. Quickly, I scanned their faces. Everyone seemed intact. Some bruises, scrapes, and other battle wounds showed on their skin, but as a whole, they were all intact.

"Good god, Hazel," Scarlett said.

"Are you alright, love?" Issa walked over to me, and I wrapped my arms around her.

"Why didn't you wake me up when you got back? I thought you all had died or something," I cried into Issa's embrace, my whole body quaking.

"We're fine, love. It was a street fight and nothing else. There were far too many people for any of us to do any real damage." She squeezed me tight and then planted a light kiss on my forehead.

"We didn't mean to worry you, little one," Caro said around bites of food. I walked over and snatched the roll right out of Caro's hand.

"Well, you did!" I stuffed the roll in my mouth and wiped my hands across my face.

"Why were you so worried?" Scarlett asked, eyeing me.

"You're my family. I don't know what I would do if something happened to one of you." I looked each of them in the eye, my heart nearly fractured at the idea of one of them being hurt beyond repair.

Scarlett's face softened, and she gave my hand a squeeze. "Saul's rowdy coven will have to do much more to get rid of us." She stroked my arm, and it sent shivers down my spine.

"Plus, they got off worse than us. Eventually, it broke up because someone called the local authorities. Those bastards know not to pick a fight with us," Naya said, sipping her coffee.

"Where do they live? I hope it's not near here. I would love it if I never had to see them again," I grumbled.

"We don't know. They don't have an established base, which is part of the problem. Tracking them is a pain in the ass. It's nearly impossible to keep tabs of where they are at any given point in time without having someone constantly on their tails." Caro sighed.

"We have protective wards around us, so they shouldn't be able to get too close to the house without us at least being alerted," Issa reassured me.

I nodded, and we all fell into a comfortable silence as we ate. It was a comfort I hadn't realized I missed. Sharing meals together was a huge deal. There were so many times I had eaten alone or not at all in an effort to keep moving and avoid people like Saul.

"Do you want to ask your questions today, Hazel?" Scarlett broke the silence, and I smiled.

"Yes, I do." I sat up straight. "I get twelve, yes?" I wanted to make sure I got the terms correct.

"Yes, darling. Twelve questions for me."

"Okay. Do you actually like me?" I blurted out. It was the first thing to come to my mind.

Scarlett threw her head back and laughed loudly, exposing her throat. I wanted to lick the honey-colored skin there.

"Of course I do. I'll do a better job of showing it, since that was your first question, darling." She touched my hand lightly and smiled playfully.

"Oh, this is good," Caro said, chuckling. Naya rolled her eyes, and Issa pulled her knees towards her chest.

"Who was your first love?" I felt more at ease knowing Scarlett's feelings were genuine and true.

"Her name was Meike. She was smart, fierce, and beautiful. We fucked each other in a barn when we were only sixteen." She had a faraway, blissful look on her face.

"How did you meet Angelica?" Most of the questions I wanted to ask were surrounding Angelica, but I wasn't sure if it would be too much. The tension in the room stayed the same as Scarlett smiled sadly.

"We were out for a night in town, and she was there, dancing and laughing in the middle of it all. It was like something out of a book. Our eyes met, and we danced throughout the evening. We were all ensnared by her beauty and charm."

I nodded. It was love at first sight.

"Are you all more powerful than Saul's coven? In magic and strength?" I asked nervously.

"I think in magic, yes, and we're smarter. I can't say in terms of brute strength, but we're more efficient." Her eyes hardened, and her lips pressed into a thin line.

"Will you continue to hunt him and eventually kill him?" I chewed my lip and looked around at the others.

"I'm not sure. It's a lot of time and energy to track him. We have tried several times to end his coven, but he always falls through our fingers." Scarlett tapped her well-manicured fingers on the table, like she was contemplating it.

"I mean, we won't turn down the opportunity, that's for sure," Nayali said, and Caro chuckled.

"Who's your favorite?" I giggled wanting to rouse the group a bit.

Scarlett broke into a wide smile. "I can't pick favorites in my family!"

"You promised me!" I whined, and she rolled her eyes. "Right now, it's you, Hazel, for being such a cheeky little thing," she said, picking up my hand and nipping at my palm. I yelped as her teeth scraped against my skin, sending heat between my thighs.

"Do you think you all want to do the ritual and share power with me?" I whispered nervously.

"Yes I do," Scarlett answered almost immediately, and it made my chest warm.

"When?"

"Very soon, I think, darling." She interlaced her fingertips in mine. I was excited for the ritual. I had been thinking about it since yesterday. My desire to be permanently a part of this family was growing each day. I didn't want anything to stand in our way.

"You only have four left. What else do you want to know, darling?"

"Can I save them? I don't know what I want to ask yet." I wanted to make them good.

"Of course you can. Feel free to ask at any time." She stood and stretched her arms over her head, exposing her soft belly. She bent down and kissed the top of my head.

"I'm exhausted and will be retiring. At dinner tonight, let's play a little bit of a game, yes?" she asked, smiling sinisterly. She looked at the others slowly, and they all said yes.

Everyone started to yawn and stretch, retiring to their beds, leaving me to my own devices. I was so grateful they were all okay.

I wanted to destroy Saul's coven. It sounded like he needed to be punished for what he had done to Angelica and what he continued to do to other mortal women.

With my free time, I headed to the library to find different ways to fight magical gifts as a mortal. I would not be caught empty handed and afraid again. I would protect my family if it was the last thing I did.

SEVENTEEN

"Are you ready for the game, Hazel?" Scarlett asked suddenly.

I nearly jumped out of my skin. "Shit, you scared me!"

Scarlett laughed and walked over to me, stroking my hair lovingly. "What are you reading up on, darling?" She ran her fingertips along the pages I was reading.

"Just getting more information on magic wielding. I don't know as much as you all, since I didn't grow up with powers. I'm just trying to understand what it all means."

She hummed behind me, and I gently closed the book, looking up into her eyes. She booped my nose, and I giggled.

"Well, we can talk more about it after we play a little, darling. Tonight, let's call it a pre-ritual for the physical task at hand. Are you ready?" She offered her hand, and I took it excitingly, already aroused.

We had all played together a little bit before, but I wanted more. There was something about satisfying all of them and them satisfying me that filled my heart and soul. It made my insides warm and happy to give them pleasure as well as take it.

Scarlett led me to the basement and explained we were heading to where the ritual would take place. We wouldn't recite the official words and do the ceremony tonight, but we would do a practice round so I knew what to expect.

"The physical ritual involves you drinking some of our essence as you make the pledge to be our fifth point. Then, we do the same to you." I nodded as we walked into the room, the others waiting for us.

A large stone table sat in the middle of the room, surrounded by four chairs. The room was a giant circle. A pentagon was painted on the floor, a fireplace roaring. Other loungers and chairs were placed on the outskirts of the room as well as some miscellaneous toys.

"First, you will please yourself as we watch. Then, you will have a turn to seduce us all and drink from our arousal. Then, we will all pleasure you together. How does that sound?" Scarlett smiled wolfishly at me, and my panties immediately dampened.

"That sounds really great."

"Undress, little one," Caro said and walked over to me, planting a kiss lightly on my knuckles.

I nodded as they led me towards the stone table.

"Do you want a toy, love? Or just your hands?" Issa asked.

"I'll use my hands tonight." I tried to sound confident, but I was a bit nervous to be on display for all of them.

"Okay, princess, get up on the table and spread those thighs when you're fully undressed," Nayali commanded. I finished stripping, all eyes on me while I climbed up on the table, the insides of my thighs already glistening.

"Gods, I can smell you from here." Caro laughed while grabbing their own toy. Nayali grabbed one too; Scarlett and Issa opted to use their own hands to watch me.

I swallowed and laid down. The stone was cold against my back. Slowly, I slid my hands over my body, warming my nipples and breasts. I moved further and dipped one finger in my already-damp pussy. I dragged my wetness up towards my nipples, and Scarlett hissed while Nayali moaned. I looked around at them, and my confidence grew as they looked at me with adoration and hunger.

I dipped another finger in and then brought it to my lips, sucking on it hard as they all groaned at the sight.

"Gods, you've got beautiful tits," Nayali said as she ground into her own toy. Slowly, they all stripped off their clothes so everyone was on display. I started circling my clit, using my other finger to pump in and out of my wet cunt. I was so turned on, it took hardly any time at all with everyone's encouraging words to come hard and fast. My back arched off the stone, and my inner walls convulsed around my fingertips.

"Crawl to me now," Scarlett commanded as I came down, and I got up and crawled on all fours over to her pretty damp lips.

"Do you devote yourself to me and this coven?" She looked at me with glittering eyes.

"Yes, I do."

"Then show me." She spread her legs wider, and her large tits bounced. I didn't need to be told twice. I put my face right in her pussy and ate her out like it was my last meal. I lapped and sucked at her clit, shoving one finger and then two inside her. A toy miraculously appeared, and she handed it to me as I pumped in and out. She commanded me to suck on her nipples and rub her clit. Scarlett cried out as she came and smashed her lips to mine, shoving her tongue into my mouth and claiming what was hers.

"Hazel."

"Yes. Go show the others how good you are at doing what you're told."

I smiled and turned around. She hit my ass with a loud slap.

"Gods, I love to watch your ass, darling. It's delicious."

Nayali was next, and she smiled at me, the gap in her teeth showing.

"Do you devote yourself to me and this coven?"

"Yes."

"Get on top of me with that wet little cunt."

I licked my lips and straddled her, letting my wetness touch her mound, sliding my fingers down to play with her clit.

"Yes, princess. Just like that. Move your hips on me," Nayali commanded, and I obeyed as she licked up the length of my neck and scraped her teeth across the delicate skin there. She bit me hard and fed. The sensation was delicious as I grinded and rode her, chasing my own climax as she shuddered beneath me.

My body was wound up so tight, I was ready to explode.

"Not yet, princess. You come again when we all devour you, and not a second sooner." She pressed her lips to mine and lifted me off her lap, squeezing my ass and sending me over to Caro.

They smiled at me as I stood in front of them, trying not to salivate at the sight of their body.

"Do you devote yourself to me and this coven?"

"Always."

"Show me what that tongue can do." Caro stood and straddled their chair so their ass was hanging off, their hole on display.

"Yes, Caro." I got on my hands and knees, swirling my tongue as Caro groaned. Gently, I slipped a finger inside them and pumped. Caro moaned as they rode my fingers and played with their clit.

"Yes, little one. A little more."

I was so turned on, I couldn't stop even if I wanted to.

Caro came around me, squeezing me and shuddering. I smiled and stood.

Caro licked up from my navel right between my breasts and planted their lips on mine. I was so shocked, they cackled and turned me towards Issa. I walked over with a goofy smile on my face.

"Do you devote yourself to me and this coven, Hazel?" Issa asked.

"Now and forever."

"Good answer." Issa commanded I sit in the chair as she slid on top of me and ordered me to suck on her tits while fingering her. It was wonderful to feel Issa's athletic body against mine, the way she writhed against my fingers in all her most vulnerable places. She clung to me as I greedily ate her tits and felt her wetness. Issa moaned my name as she fell apart in my hands. She dipped one finger into me and then back out, and I gasped, wanting to feel a release with all this tension built up.

I was going mad pleasuring my beloveds, and I wanted to release this wave of desire inside me.

"Drink some water, darling, and have a snack. We want you hydrated and fed for what we have in store," Scarlett commanded.

I obeyed and let Issa clean me up, Caro feeding me while Nayali fetched water. I was buzzing with anticipation, but I did what I was told. When I had drank and eaten enough to satisfy everyone, Nayali clapped her hands.

"Now, let's begin the next part, princess. You ask each of us if we are devoted to you and if we trust you to hold our powers. Do you understand?' Nayali guided me over to the stone tablet.

"Yes."

"Then let's begin, little one." Caro helped me up.

And the rest of the practice ritual began.

EIGHTEEN

I laid down on the table, and it lowered so I was accessible for everyone to touch and stroke. They took turns teasing me with their fingertips and tongues, never getting to any of the aching parts, like my breasts, pussy or mouth. They stayed along my fingertips, arms, and legs.

"Spread your legs." Issa guided my thighs wide as she climbed up on the table. She inhaled my pussy, and I nearly came on the spot.

"You ready?" I nodded, not being able to speak as the others gathered around. Issa dived in with her mouth, and I cried out as she sucked and tongue fucked me. Caro and Nayali descended on my breasts as Scarlett leaned over and consumed me with her pillowy lips. I was so full of sensation and pleasure from all of them, it was almost too much.

I wanted to milk this out as long as possible, but my body gave out as warmth rushed through me. I came all over Issa's face in a scream swallowed by Scarlett's sweet mouth.

"You're delicious, Hazel." Issa wiped her mouth and smiled at me as I panted from the most mind boggling orgasm I ever had.

"My turn," Nayali said while she wrapped a strap on around her waist and settled in front of my swollen pussy. She eased the dildo in, and immediately, my body squeezed around it. Issa climbed on top of me and sat on my face. I ate her hungrily as Nayali thrust into me, playing with my clit, Scarlett and Caro devouring my aching nipples, my body practically on fire.

I was so consumed with sensations, I didn't know what to do. The pleasure built quick and fast as Nayali thrust into me, and I convulsed around her. I sucked Issa's clit, and pride shuddered through me when she also cried out. Nayali slipped out of me, and Issa hopped off, kissing my mouth.

"We taste good together." She winked.

"How did you like that, princess?" Nayali asked, and I was nearly speechless again. The ways in which my body could be used for my coven seemed limitless.

"That was magical," I panted. Caro took the strap on and wrapped it around their body.

"Now, on all fours, little one. You'll eat Scarlett's pussy while Nayali and Issa ravish those beautiful breasts of yours."

It was like a dance. Everyone knew their place for optimal pleasure. The stone table suddenly had openings for my heavy tits to plop into as Caro eased into my ass and then played with my clit. Scarlett positioned her wet folds in front of me, and I devoured her. They all tasted so different and delicious, and I couldn't get enough.

I felt stretched and wonderfully used as Caro worked my asshole and the others worked my breasts. Scarlett gripped my hair and moved against my tongue. It was all too easy to eat their pleasure and then crash into my own. The free fall of pleasure was deep and all-consuming as I shuddered around Caro and groaned into Scarlett's wet pussy.

"One more, darling," Scarlett said as Caro eased out of me.

"Stay on all fours and move towards the edge."

Ass propped up, I worked it back until Scarlett started eating me from behind as the others took turns with my mouth and my tits.

I was a live wire. All my senses were firing, and I was sure I would die of happiness. It was a beautiful cornucopia of orgasms and love. I wanted to stay like this forever. I came hard and fast in what felt like a blink of an eye.

I collapsed on the stone table, breathing hard and nearly limp.

Caro scooped me up from the table, and it slid into the ground. I was carried to a shower, where Caro lovingly cleaned every part of me. The others joined in, touching and trading kisses with me while they too washed up.

Finally, Nayali deposited me on a giant bed, where they snuggled around me, settling in together.

"Sleep, little one. You worked hard tonight," Caro said.

"It's time to dream, darling," Scarlett whispered.

"Close your eyes," Issa said.

"Sweet dreams," Nayali finished, and I drifted off into a sex-and-love-induced haze.

I woke up the next morning with arms and legs wrapped around me, the scent of sex in the air. It was intoxicating.

"What did you think of last night?" Caro asked, turning to me and kissing my nose.

"It was the most amazing thing I have ever experienced." I meant it, too. I never knew there could be pleasure like that. I was flying on cloud nine.

"It was pretty orgasmic." Issa giggled from where she stood at the end of the bed, already dressed.

"How long have we been sleeping?"

"Not long. You needed the rest." Nayali walked in, also dressed, with a plate of food in hand.

"Where's Scarlett?"

Caro and I were the only ones in the bed.

"She went to take care of something, but she'll be back soon," Caro said, patting my hand and encouraging me to eat.

I nodded and dug right in, not realizing how hungry I was. We ate and laughed together, all in desperate need of nutrients after our marathon of sex.

"I was preparing for the magic part of the ritual." Scarlett floated in, and I perked up.

"Yes! I'm ready to know all about it. Last night was just practice for the real thing, right? So when will we do the actual ritual?" I asked greedily.

"Soon, darling. Some things need to be put in place before we can proceed." Scarlett looked lovingly at me.

"And we shall talk about the ritual, but we won't do a practice round. We will simply complete it after the physical part is done."

I nodded, wondering why we couldn't just get to doing it sooner rather than later. What needed to happen before we could become a real, true coven?

"In the meantime, we will each be having another day with you to talk about our specific powers and tell you a bit more about what it means to be the fifth point." Caro grabbed a grape and popped it into their mouth.

"That sounds fun! Who is going first?"

"I will, darling," Scarlett said, and my insides grew warm.

"Today or tomorrow?" I asked.

"Tomorrow. Today is for eating and sleeping! No sex today," she commanded. I pouted, and they all laughed. I was tired, but I could always go for more. So, we spent the rest of the day relaxing and enjoying each other's company. It was the best day I had in a very long time.

Nineteen

"Darling, it's time to wake." Scarlett gently stroked my arm and let her fingertips rest on my cheek. I nuzzled into her palm.

"Is it time already?" I hummed without opening my eyes. Her fingers felt warm against my skin.

"Yes. I'm going to show you what my magic can do, Hazel."

I sat up quickly. Scarlett sat next to me, lounging along the length of the bed. Her curves were on full display, and she smiled, her red lips looking delicious enough to eat.

"You look breathtaking." I tried not to drool or notice the heat pooling between my thighs.

"And you look wonderfully rumpled. Shall we make both of us a little more disheveled?" She climbed on top of me and pulled her breasts out, thrusting one into my mouth. I sucked greedily. Her tits were beautiful, and I would happily stay underneath her all day.

She shifted, and I whined when her nipple escaped my lips and she replaced it with her mouth. I wrapped my legs around her waist and pressed myself into her softness. She moved to my neck, and I shivered as her lips captured my own peaks.

I groaned as heat pooled between my thighs. She reached down to finger fuck me, circling my clit with her thumb and pumping one finger inside me. I writhed against her, my climax already building aggressively. She nipped and licked across my breasts, and I was simply putty in her hands. Scarlett took her mouth lower and lower until she was right at my soaking wet pussy.

"My favorite breakfast." She licked her lips and pulled her red hair back as she pushed her hands underneath my ass. In one hard pull, my wet cunt was in her mouth. She dove in, eating me out like she was starving for my taste.

I moaned her name as she tongue fucked me. She licked along my seam, dipping her fingers in and out as an orgasm crashed into me. I shivered with pleasure as Scarlett kissed along my thighs, moving back to my mouth and shoving her tongue in. It was a claim. I was hers and she was mine.

"Can I have you too?" I whispered against her, and she laughed a light, twinkling sound.

"I wish you would, darling. Make Mommy come," she commanded. My body moved before my mind fully understood. Scarlett sat leisurely against the pillows, spreading her legs wide and exposing her pussy, hot and ready for me.

I licked my lips and settled between her legs, looking up at her. Her thick body was a work of art, and she nodded encouragingly. My lips danced across her hips, and I nibbled at her thighs until she grabbed my head and shoved my mouth right to her clit. It was rough in the best possible way. I sucked and lapped at her wetness, groaning into her pretty little cunt.

Her taste was glorious, and she set the pace, the pressure of her hands demanding I add more fingers. My name fell from her lips while she rode my face until she cried out, shuddering around me. I smiled into her cunt, proud of myself for bringing her so much pleasure.

She dragged me up, and I straddled her as she guided me to her breasts again. A breathy sigh escaped her mouth as I sucked and nibbled on her luscious tits. Her pleasure was on full display, and I wanted to bask in it all day long. Once she made herself come again, she used her own wetness to finger fuck me until I was squirming around her, climaxing yet again.

"How do you like that for a morning wake up call, Hazel?" She snuggled into my neck, and I giggled.

"I like it a lot. Can I ask one of my unused questions?" I nervously posed as I twiddled my thumbs.

Scarlett looked surprised and lifted her brow. "Sure, darling. What's your question?"

"If I said I love you, would you say it back?" I looked everywhere but her face, afraid of the answer. I knew I loved her and the others; I just didn't know if they felt the same.

She gently put a finger underneath my chin and lifted my eyes to meet hers.

"I would say I love you too, darling. You belong to this coven, and us to you." The answer was sealed with a demanding kiss that made my insides go liquid again.

"Say it again, Hazel," she commanded with a smile.

"I love you, Scarlett." My belly erupted in a million butter-flies as my smile grew to match hers.

"And I love you, Hazel." She stroked my cheek lovingly, and it felt like the sun was on my skin.

"Now, my darling, we have to get out of bed so I can show you my magic and how it will be shared and used with you as the conduit. Are you ready to see what the day has in store?" Standing, she slipped on a black dress with thigh high slits and a plunging neckline.

"Yes. I can be ready in just a minute!" I said excitedly as I hurried around, freshening up and throwing on some clothes. Scarlett fetched a basket of food for us to take to the forest for a picnic so we could talk about her magic.

It was no time at all before we found ourselves on the forest floor, cross legged snacking, and talking while the sun shone down on us.

"Alright, darling. The base of my magic is spell casting. It is less tied to the elements than the fae, more like special tricks. It can be offensive, defensive, or something in between. I can throw attack spells or create a defensive shield. I will show you."

She whispered unfamiliar words and put on a display, showing all different kinds of skills. Things blasted in different colors, things popped and crackled, static electricity sizzling in the air.

"You must have had to memorize a lot of spells to be able to make this all work." I watched as she moved and twisted her hands while she chanted.

"I did. The words and actions must be precise to have the most impact. However, when you get involved with the sharing of power, the words do not need to be spoken. Strong intent should do the trick. So, if Naya needed a shield, you could channel my power to her without words. It would be like you borrowed from what I can already produce. Does that make sense?"

I nodded, thinking of how that would be useful. I could be the thing that held us together in times of danger. I could share everyone's power in a way that made things easier. We would need to train, but we would have the ability to protect one another with the simplest thought.

"It makes us very powerful, which is why it is such a coveted affair. If we can establish our physical and mental links seamlessly, you will be able to spread and disperse power in ways that are quite formidable." She looked wistfully up at the sky.

"Our family would be a force to be reckoned with. We would be able to protect one another through thick and thin." The thought brought me great comfort.

"It is a delicate balance of power that must be protected and nurtured, darling. It takes a special person to be a fifth point, and I believe, with my whole heart, it was always meant to be you." She grabbed my hand, intertwining our fingers naturally.

"Will we be able to do the ritual now, or do I still need to do something else?" I asked, looking at our fingers.

"I believe after your days with each of the others, we will have what we need to move forward, darling. For love is the only way." She winked at me and I think I finally understood.

Love needed to be shared between all of us for it to happen. I knew I loved the others, but did they love me? I wasn't sure.

"Do not worry, darling. All you have to do is ask." Scarlett smiled warmly at me, and with that, the rest of the day was ours to play.

TWENTY

"Princess, are you ready to play?" Naya sat across from me while I finished my breakfast.

"With you, Naya? I'm always ready to play," I teased, feeling light and airy this morning after the day I had with Scarlett.

"Did you have a good day with Scar yesterday?" Naya popped a grape in her mouth, and I saw a flash of the metal stud on her tongue.

"I did. It was quite pleasurable." I blushed, and Naya laughed.

"Shall I show you what I can do with my powers today as well, Hazel?"

"Yes, I would very much like to see." Naya reached for my hand, and we headed out of the house to an open field.

"Now, as a vampire, I have speed and strength that are nearly unmatched. My instincts are heightened, and so are my senses. Not quite as much as Caro's, but nearly so without the animal form." I nodded, watching Naya move through the field.

She would jump and run like the wind carried her. It was

magnificent to see her body move and weave with grace and power.

"So I can lend that capacity to others?" I wondered what of her powers could be shared in the binding of our coven.

"Yes, princess. You can lend someone extra speed, strength, agility, or even healing abilities, as I heal rather quickly. Not as fast as Issa, but still quick." She winked at me. There were many advantages to each of their powers, and I would need to know them inside and out.

"That's truly magnificent. We will surely be the most powerful coven there is, and I have only seen what you and Scar can do thus far." I looked at Naya in amazement.

"If you look at me like that much longer, princess, I will have to do something about it..." She winked, and the heat went straight to my belly.

"What if I wanted you to do something about it?" I walked up to her and wrapped my arms around her luscious waist.

"I haven't fed from you today...." She ran her nose up the column of my throat, and I shivered at the feel of my nipples pebbling.

"Will you please?" I whispered against her skin, and she spun me around. Her breasts pushed into my back as she licked up the sides of my throat, palming my tits.

"You're already turned on, princess?" She chuckled in my ear, and goosebumps broke out across my skin.

"I'm always turned on by you, Naya," I responded huskily as her fingers started their journey to the band of my pants. Her fingers explored my wet center as I melted against her.

"Are you, princess?" She pulled her fingertips out and sucked on them one by one as I shivered against her.

"Naya," I practically begged as she began to kiss along my throat. She plunged her fingers inside me as she clamped her fangs down on my skin, drinking in long pulls from my neck.

It was the most erotic feeling to have her both feeding and fucking me. Her teeth and tongue soothed as she drank, and heat raced through my blood as I cried out. My orgasm ripped through me, my body coming apart while she lapped at the puncture wounds on my neck.

I hung limply in her arms, and she turned me around so her lips could find mine. We tangled our tongues. In one, swift movement, she lifted me so I could wrap my legs around her. Gently, she placed me on the ground, taking no time at all to whip her trousers off. Her glistening pussy quickly came to rest on my face, and my mouth knew exactly what to do, sucking and lapping at her arousal. The need for her to feel as I did was so strong. All I wanted was to please her.

I wanted to drown in her pleasure. I want to be the reason she could live and breathe with my blood coursing through her veins. She rode my mouth as I grabbed her ass and pressed my face deeper into her cunt. She detonated around me, her inner walls tightening while she ground against my lips. When her climax ran its course, she dismounted my face and laid beside me, our lips meeting once more. The taste was of her arousal and my blood mixed with something deliciously ours.

"Naya, can I ask you something?" I wanted to make sure.

"Yes, Hazel, of course."

"It's one of my last three questions."

Naya looked at me quizzically. "Ask away."

"Do you love me?" I found the courage to search her eyes, watery from emotions.

"I do. I love you very much." She kissed me slowly, seductively, and I melted in her arms.

"I love you too," I whispered against her mouth.

We smiled at one another, our foreheads touching. Kisses were traded back and forth for a long time before we both settled.

"Scarlett said that was the last piece of this puzzle," I finally said as the sun started to set.

"She told you?" Naya sounded surprised.

"In so many words. I used one of my last questions to ask her what she would say if I told her I loved her. She said she would say it back. All I had to do was ask the questions of the others to make our coven complete."

Naya smiled widely. "That sounds like something she would do, princess. Do you feel satisfied with your answers thus far?"

"I do. I'm nervous about the others; it is scary to love after all these years of distrust and running. It's hard to be vulnerable—it means there is so much more to lose," I confessed.

"I know. Love can be both wonderful and terrifying, but you are ours and we are yours. Do not ever forget that, princess. You complete us in a way no one else possibly could. It has always been you." Her hands stroked my cheeks, tears filling my eyes.

"But Angelica?" I didn't want to be rude, but I wanted to know if they had the same connection to her.

"Maybe, but we never found out. We cared for Angelica deeply, but perhaps she was never going to be the fifth point and you were always going to be it. You need not compare yourself to her, princess. The past is the past, and our hearts are yours."

I snuggled in closer, and we stayed there until the sun went down and the stars came alive. We gazed up at the sky, and I couldn't help but wonder what would be in store when I asked the others if love was in their hearts.

TWENTY-ONE

I was still reeling from the past two days with Naya and Scarlett. I couldn't believe they both had said they loved me. Love had always felt so elusive, so far away. I had no idea that it could be like this—expansive and without limits, with several people who were my chosen ones.

"Guess who?" a voice said from behind me as hands covered my eyes. I had been sitting in one of the gardens, reading a book, unsure of how to find time with Caro and Issa. It seemed like I didn't have to think too much about it, though, because I knew that voice anywhere.

"Caro." I giggled and shut my book before prying their hands from my eyes.

"Good guess, little one." They plopped down in front of me, smiling broadly. "What are you reading?" Caro grabbed the book from where I had tossed it and opened to a random page.

"Just a little romance book." I blushed thinking about the passages I had been reading. It was right in the middle of the main characters making passionate love.

"Oh, little one. This is a good book indeed." Caro scanned

the pages hungrily, and I knew it had to be on an extremely explicit part. What perfect timing.

"You can borrow it when I'm done." I tried to snatch it out of their hands, but they were too fast, pulling it away at the last second. I sprawled over their lap, trying to grab the book.

"This feels almost exactly like the book." Caro looked down at me with a gleam in their eyes, and it instantly made my thighs slick. My ass was up, my chest pressed against their strong thighs.

"Caro," I breathed.

"I think you need a little punishment, little one." Caro hiked my long skirt up my thighs, exposing my black lace thong. "Oh, what a pretty little scrap of fabric." Caro snapped my panties against my skin, leaving a sting behind. I yelped in anticipation of what was going to happen next.

"Have you been bad, little one?" Caro purred, massaging the globes of my ass. The movement made my pussy ache for their touch.

"Yes." I wanted Caro to punish me—*badly*.

"That's what I thought." Caro dipped a finger between my thighs and stroked my seam. I groaned and writhed against them, but their other arm came down to keep me firmly in place across their lap.

"Not yet, little one." Caro massaged my bare ass and then spanked me. *Hard*. The zing of pain made everything ache even more.

I squirmed and squeaked as they returned to rubbing. My pussy clenched on nothing as my thong became even more soaked.

"Did you like that, little one? You like being naughty?" Caro purred.

"Yes."

Caro followed with another loud smack, and I groaned as

they slipped a finger into me. A delicious dichotomy of sensations, the fullness of their fingers inside my pussy, the sting of my bare ass was all intoxicating.

Suddenly, Caro's mouth was on the spot they had just hit as they bit into the skin, hard. It was a piercing sensation of pleasure as they started licking and sucking. I groaned and arched my spine, wanting more while their mouth moved closer to my puckered hole.

Several sensations happened at once: Caro's hot mouth pressed against me while their fingers explored my innermost walls, the stinging of my backside adding to the ecstasy I felt. My orgasm started to build, hard and fast. Screaming, I crashed into it, squirming and writhing in their lap. My breath nearly gone, I laid there until the sensations subsided, and they gently flipped me over, smiling down at me.

"How'd that feel, little one?" they asked.

"Amazing." I crawled off their lap as they shed their pants and spread their legs wide for me to dive in.

"Show me how much you liked it," Caro commanded, and I dove into their own pleasure, licking and sucking, using my mouth, tongue, and fingertips to coax the same sensations out of Caro they had elicited from me. I could have stayed there for hours, but almost immediately, they were fucking my face before coming all over me.

"God, you're irresistible," Caro said, stroking my hair.

"So are you." I meant it, too. "Caro, can I ask you something?" I was feeling bold and wanted to ask before I lost the courage.

"Yes, little one?"

I sat up so we faced one another. "Do you...do you love me?"

Caro broke out into a grin. "I sure do, little one. I love you a whole lot."

I gasped and flung myself at them.

"I will take that to mean you love me too?" they laughed. I cried into their shirt and hugged them like I couldn't imagine letting them go.

"Yes, I love you too!"

"I'll show you how much," Caro said wolfishly as we went for another round of showing each other how much we cared for one another.

Several orgasms, showers, and snacks later, we made it out into the surrounding meadows so Caro could show me their power.

"As a shifter, I turn fully into any animal I'm familiar with." Caro showed me how they switched between a bear, a cheetah, an elephant, even dogs, cats, and birds.

"So what's the limitation of shifting?" I wanted to make sure I fully understood.

"I need to know a decent amount about the animal—the name and species of it, how it looks to focus my magic to make it manifest in my body."

I nodded. "How can that be used in our coven when we share the magical connection?"

"I can lend my shifter animal to anyone for a short period of time, about sixty seconds."

"That is so cool!" I squealed.

"It is time-limited, as I can only share it while I'm also still in my shifter form, so it must be used wisely and precisely."

For the rest of the day, Caro showed me more animals. Only one more to go, and Issa was the one who I had the most confidence in. I just hoped I wasn't too arrogant. I wanted this to be my coven, and I would do anything to make that happen.

TWENTY-TWO

"You seem very nervous, love." Issa and I were having tea, and my nerves were all over the place. The frantic energy inside me threatened to shove me out of my seat. For some reason, this one was the hardest. Issa and I were the first to connect, and somehow, that made this even harder.

"I'm nervous," I confessed, taking a small sip of my tea. My hands were shaking, and I nearly dropped my drink.

"Do you want to talk about it?" Issa steadied my hand and gave my fingers a squeeze.

"Kind of. I have one question."

Issa looked at me quizzically, and then realization hit her features. "Ah, from

Scarlett's questions. You only have one left?"

I nodded, chewing my lip. "Yes, just one."

"And how did you use the other ones? You had four left, if I remember correctly." Issa smiled like she had a secret. I just knew she had the answer already.

"You know what the questions were, I think," I said softly.

"Yes, love, but I want to hear it from your own lips."

"Well, I asked Scarlett, Naya, and Caro if they loved me." I twisted my fingers. "And what were their answers, my love?" Issa took another small sip.

"They all said they loved me, and I said I loved them back." I broke out into a huge grin.

"And the final question you have today is for me?"

I shrugged. "Will you make me ask it, even though you already know?"

"I think I would like to hear the question, just in case I'm wrong," Issa teased.

"Fine!" I giggled. "Issa, I love you. Will you say it and mean it back?" I asked.

"Of course, my love. I love you. I have loved you from the very beginning, and I am ready for our coven to be complete with you as the glue that holds us all together. Come here." She patted her lap, and I didn't need to be told twice as I straddled her in her seat.

"You were the first one I knew for sure. How funny that I was the most nervous to tell you," I whispered against her mouth, our foreheads touching.

"Sometimes, the first is the hardest, Hazel," Issa whispered back. Then, our mouths were touching, our tongues tangled in a sweet, slow rhythm, like we could be here all day and never get tired of each other's soft lips.

Wetness started to pool between my thighs, and Issa reached down to play with my clit. I widened my legs, and she did the same with hers as we dove into the other's wet pussy, playing and twirling as our mouths devoured one another. Our orgasms practically arrived in sync. I clung to her as we shuddered and moaned. Together, we erupted.

"God, I love you," I panted.

"And I love you too," she answered, planting another kiss against my lips. "Now, let me show you what power will be shared. How about that?" I nodded while we both straightened ourselves out and headed outside.

We walked hand in hand out to the forest, and Issa sat me down.

"Okay, so fae magic is like small pieces of all the others—magic more elemental, no spell casting, enhanced physical attributes, though not entirely animal-like and not as intense as Vampires. Additionally, I have the ability to portal, which will be very useful in combat and can be lended to others."

I nodded. "Okay, I think I understand that."

Issa showed me how her magic worked, how she could command energy, but it wasn't quite as showy as Scarlett's. Then, we practiced portaling together from the house and back to the forest. My brain felt like scrambled eggs, but it was making sense to me. We spent several hours outside until the sun dipped down and the stars started to peak out.

"I think it's time we go inside, love," Issa said as the last sliver of light left for the evening.

———

"Did you solve the puzzle, darling?" Scarlett asked while we all settled inside to eat.

"I did. You said love was the only way, and love is what we have. Is that the final piece? We needed love to make this complete?" I chewed thoughtfully.

"Yes. The words needed to be spoken to complete the full ritual. Covens were always meant to be havens and support for all those involved. Over the years, it has developed into something violating and malicious for some, so I wanted to make sure we felt it here." She tapped her heart.

"Well, I couldn't be happier to be here with my beloveds." I gave them a goofy smile.

"We are glad to have you here too, little one," Caro said.

"Now, we can move to the ritual in the next day or two. We need to make a few other preparations, but otherwise, we are good to go, princess," Naya said. I practically bounced in my seat.

"I'm so excited to make it official."

"A toast to our coven, now complete with our lovely Hazel." Issa held up a glass, and so did the others. We all cheered and drank, laughing and enjoying one another's company.

I couldn't imagine anything dulling our shine. I was ready to pledge myself to them and them to me. I couldn't wait for tomorrow to come.

TWENTY-THREE

I was buzzing with excitement when I woke up. Today was the day we would begin the rituals, and I was beyond ready for what was in store. The sun shone through my curtains and seemed to say hello. Dressing quickly, I hurried to put on comfortable clothes and headed to the breakfast table.

Scarlett and Caro were already there, smiling at me when I walked in.

"Good morning." I stopped by Scarlett and planted a light kiss on her cheek then did the same to Caro.

"Good morning, Hazel." Scarlett patted my cheek.

"Good morning, little one." Caro passed me some food.

"Are the others not up yet?" I buttered some toast and continued to fill my plate.

"Issa was training this morning, and Naya was just rising," Scarlett answered, sipping her coffee.

"Feeling anxious to get today started, little one?" Caro teased, and I nodded.

"I'm so ready! It feels like the most natural thing in the world to do." My knee bounced underneath the table.

"Soon, darling. First, you need to eat and hydrate—it will be a long day." Scarlett laughed, and I rolled my eyes.

Issa and Naya finally joined us, and our little coven was in the same space again. There was something special about us all being together. I could feel the power and connection we shared whenever we were all in the same orbit. Did the others feel it too, or was it just me?

Breakfast seemed to drag on forever until, finally, the chatter and laughter died down. I looked at all of them expectantly.

"Someone is very excited." Naya eyed me.

"Hazel is more than ready to take the oath and the commitment." Issa stood and reached out for my hand.

"Can we begin?" I stood abruptly and grabbed her fingertips.

"Let's begin, darling." Scarlett chuckled, and we made our way into the lower levels of the estate.

"First, we will share a mark." Issa said as we trailed down stone steps through corridors. I tried to concoct a mental map of where we were, but my brain was too anxious.

"Will we share tattoos?" I giggled. That sounded fun.

"Yes. A pentagram on each of us, with the five points being the letter of our first name, with some words spoken to seal the deal," Caro explained.

We ended up in a room already set up with the tools needed for the mark and plush chairs for us to sit in.

Carefully, we each reached for our own needles under Issa's direction. She said they had been spelled to create the perfect pentagram once they made contact with our skin. We all watched in silent awe as the needles moved our hands of their own volition.

"Now, we each write our initials on one another's skin. I'll go first." Issa wrote an I on all our wrists at one of the points.

"I shall go next," Naya said. Each of us kept a serious

expression despite the sting of the ink, followed by Scarlett and Caro.

"Now me?" I asked, and they all nodded. I tried to take great care to write the H on the last point available.

"Now, we chant together. "To the coven, we are devoted, until death do us part. Our beloved hearts are here to stay, with no one else shall we be permitted to play." Issa smiled and winked at me on the last part.

I giggled as we chanted the words, and the ink sizzled and burned into our flesh before a light whispered across everyone's skin. I reached and touched the mark, now smooth on my flesh.

"The ritual has begun," Issa said seriously.

"Step one is complete." Caro ran their fingers over their ink.

"What is step two?" I asked.

"We give a little of our magic to one another through you, Hazel. We will each give you a drop of our power, and you will give it to the others. It all starts with a kiss. A little bit of witchcraft." Scarlett held my face in her hands and kissed me deeply. Her pillowy soft lips commanded mine and made my panties wet. It felt like it lasted forever and simultaneously not long enough.

"A little bit of shifting." Caro stepped up after Scarlett and commanded me with teeth and tongue. It was such a possessive kiss, it made my knees weak.

"Now, a little bit of fae magic." Issa pulled me into her and laid one on me. She bit and nibbled softly, pulling at my bottom lip, making me moan.

"Finally, some vampiric energy." Naya bit hard and drew a little blood before her tongue thrusted into my mouth, laying claim to what was hers.

They each loved differently and beautifully. I was fully

infatuated with all of them. I could feel the tingly bits of magic at my lips, like I had just eaten something spicy.

"Now, kiss each of our tattoos," Caro said. Everyone held out their arms, and I pressed light kisses to each of their wrists. It was a simple moment, but it felt like the most intimate thing we had ever done together.

"Yours too," Naya commanded, and I pressed my lips to my own wrist, feeling a little heat there.

"That's it?" I said. I could feel the whisper of power and connection to all of them as our coven bonds started to fall into place.

"Yes. Each coven can customize their own magical ritual, and this one seemed to make the most sense for us. Someone like Saul would make it more rough and less intimate," Scarlett said disdainfully.

"You will start to feel and almost visualize the coven bonds in your heart. We will always be reached, no matter how far apart, but we will practice all of that later. Today is for the ritual, and we will practice how to use the bonds tomorrow," Issa said.

"How do you feel, little one?" Caro asked, and I smiled.

"I feel great. Ready for more," I giggled.

"Then let's get to it," Naya said.

We all stood to leave the tattoo room and head to the physical ritual. I tried to quiet the butterflies in my belly, but they couldn't be contained. I wanted to promise myself fully and physically to them. It was all my heart desired.

TWENTY-FOUR

"Are you ready, little one?" Caro asked while they led me to the stone table from the last pre-ritual.

I nodded. "Yes."

"You know what's first," Caro said.

I stripped down, feeling more confident than ever looking at my loved ones around me.

Scarlett moved chairs with a whispered spell, and they all surrounded the table. I walked over to the toys and decided on one that vibrated.

"I'm going to use this one today," I declared.

"Aw, look how our princess has grown!" Naya chuckled.

"You're stepping into your own comfort, love." Issa looked lovingly at me.

With a deep breath, I walked up to the table once more and lied down, my toy next to me. I began to touch myself, stroking my nipples, palming my breasts. My fingertips traveled lower to my pussy, already aching for attention. I dipped my fingers in and circled my clit, sending heat across my lower abdomen.

"That's it, little one," Caro growled next to me, watching

intently. Today, no one was touching themselves in response. Instead, they were fixated on me. Naya licked her lips, and Issa narrowed her eyes.

I grabbed the phallic-like toy and turned it on, stroking my clit and dipping it inside me. Slowly, I pumped it in and out, grinding against it, trying to chase my orgasm, desperately wishing it was one of the others making me come.

I groaned as the orgasm shot through me.

"Such a lovely sound." Scarlett chewed her lip.

"Now, come here, little one." Caro stripped off their pants, and I scrambled over to them.

"Do you devote yourself to me and this coven?" Caro asked, their gaze heated.

"Yes." I dropped to my knees and dove between their legs, trying to imprint the taste and smell of Caro on my mind and my tongue. Caro fucked my face ferociously, like they were an animal unleashed and I was simply along for the ride.

"Fuck!" Caro gasped as they quaked and shivered around me.

"Go devote yourself to the others," Caro commanded, pulling my lips to theirs in a rough kiss.

"Come to me, love," Issa beckoned. "Do you devote yourself to me and this coven?"

"Yes."

The air was serious, the ritual winding its magic. It was the feeling of us, laced with power and love. I dropped to my knees in front of Issa and looked up at her expectantly.

"You're beautiful, love. Keep going. You're doing fantastic."

I smiled and licked her hot center, reveling in the essence of her. Caro had been fast and furious while Issa was slow, with controlled power. She rolled her hips against my lips as I pumped my fingers inside her. She came in a slow moan while she rode my tongue through her orgasm.

Issa sealed it with a kiss and squeezed my butt, pushing me back to the others.

"Join me, darling," Scarlett said, beckoning me over. "Do you devote yourself to me and the coven?"

I nodded. "Yes."

She pushed my head towards her pussy, and I inhaled deeply. Scarlett was in charge as she thrust her hips to my lips. I licked and sucked hungrily at her, wanting to be filled with her arousal. I could simply live in this moment forever.

"Right there, darling." Scarlett gripped my hair and kept me moving until she arched her back and moaned against me. Once her orgasm subsided, she roughly dragged me up and licked across my lips.

"God, I love the taste of us together. Now go see Naya."

"Come to me, princess." Naya opened her arms. "Do you devote yourself to me and this coven?"

"Yes."

Naya lowered me down to her pussy. There was something wonderful about mixing their scents in my nose and their tastes on my tongue. She seemed content to let me take my time as her fingers brushed through my hair.

I sucked and licked, wanting to give her all the pleasure in the world, just like the others. Soon, she was writhing and moaning until she exploded over my tongue.

"Hazel," she breathed.

I stood, my body bare to all of them. Slowly, everyone stripped off any remaining clothing, and soon, we all stood there, open and vulnerable to each other.

"You did good, Hazel." Scarlett caressed my cheek.

"Let's clean you up, and then we'll finish the rest of this ritual and set the final bonds."

They walked me over to the shower and took turns running soap across my body and scrubbing my hair thoughtfully. Every moment was intimate and full of love. It made my heart swell.

They helped me out of the shower, and multiple hands ran over me with lotion and a brush.

"I love you all," I said, looking at each of them individually.

"And we love you." Issa placed a kiss on my forehead.

"Are you ready to finish the rest of the ritual?" Naya grabbed my hand.

"Yes, I want to make this permanent." I touched the tattoo on the inside of my wrist—I meant it.

"Then let's finish what we started, little one," Caro said. It was time to cement my love in my bones and my heart.

The stone table lay before me, and I stepped up, taking a deep breath. Slowly, I lied down on the cold surface, and the others gathered around me. Each touched some part of my skin, sending heat straight to my core.

"I'm ready." I beamed at each of them, the magic creating goosebumps on my skin and tingling in my chest. I wanted this so bad, to finally have a family, a home. This was where I needed to be.

TWENTY-FIVE

"Relax, darling," Scarlett purred in my ear as she trailed kisses across my collarbone. Naya and Issa were on either side of me, their fingertips and lips fanning across my skin. One would capture a nipple and the other would bite hard. It was a delicious cacophony of sensations.

Caro settled between my legs, my thighs over their shoulders as they licked up and down the soft flesh. My pussy was slick with arousal, and I desperately wanted Caro to taste me. Scarlett's lips found mine and held me steady as Caro began to explore.

I felt pressure at my puckered hole and cold lubrication as Caro gently pressed into my tightness. My entire body felt full and deliciously warm. Pleasure rolled through me as the sensations took over. Caro dove in, licking and sucking at my clit as they fingered my ass.

The ecstasy built in my belly as Caro tongue fucked me, and the others found the other pleasure points on the inside of my wrists, neck, and breasts. I groaned into Scarlett's mouth while my orgasm ripped through me.

"Caro," I breathed, bucking my hips and pressing myself

into their face. They clamped a hand down on my thigh and milked out the last remaining bits of my climax.

"Delicious," Caro growled, and everyone rotated so Issa was positioned between my thighs. Caro and Scarlett flanked me while Naya stroked my hair.

"Naya, will you be a gem and mount Hazel?" Issa bit my inner thigh, and I yelped in delight. Naya climbed on top of me and straddled my face, her pussy ready to be devoured. Issa bit against my hip, sending heat across my skin.

It was rough in the yummiest way. I sucked harder on Naya's clit as Issa fingered me before licking me from front to back. She alternated her tasks, and it took no time at all for me to become a mewling mess.

"Come for me, love," Issa commanded, and I shuddered underneath her. Naya and I rushed off the cliff towards our relief, falling off the cliff together. I shivered and convulsed on the table, pleasure shooting down to my toes.

"What a good girl." Naya patted my cheek and wiped her essence from my face as Issa kissed the inside of my knee.

"God, you all are going to kill me," I said, trying to catch my breath as Caro brought me some water.

"Drink up, little one. You still have two more to go, minimum."

I gulped greedily and looked around. Fuck, I was so in love.

"Are you okay to keep going?" Scarlett asked, stroking my arms.

"Yes, please." I lied back down, and they all settled around me once more. This time, Scarlett occupied the space between my thighs, Caro at my mouth. Scarlett picked up a few toys and gently pushed a vibrating one into me while she licked at my clit.

Caro gently nipped and licked at my throat and ears, never settling fully on my mouth. The others teased my nipples but never with enough friction for me to come. I writhed on the table for what felt like hours. Scarlett drew out all the deepest sensations until, finally, she stayed on my clit long enough to elicit a mind-blowing orgasm. It exploded through me all the way down to my toes.

I cried out, my back arching off the stone table as she milked every last drop of pleasure from me.

"Good, darling. You can do one more for, Naya."

They rotated once more, and I was breathless. I didn't know if I could give another one.

"Can I feed from you, princess?" Naya looked at me with hungry eyes, and I grew wet once more.

"Yes," I panted.

The others went to work as Naya placed little nibbles along my body. Nayali lifted my legs, biting into the fleshy part of my ass while pumping her fingers in and out of my pussy. I cried out as white hot pain oozed into warm pleasure, the orgasm exploded from me while she fed. Another climax overtook me when her mouth met my clit and her hands massaged my ass.

"Holy fuck," I panted.

Naya gently settled my legs and backside down, and I lay fully spent on the stone table. They each came and kissed me lovingly.

"I devote myself to you and my power to the coven," Issa said after kissing me once more.

"I devote myself to you and my power to the coven," Caro whispered and nuzzled my neck.

"I devote myself to you and my power to the coven." Naya rubbed her nose against mine.

"I devote myself to you and my power to the coven," Scarlett finished by kissing each cheek and then my mouth.

"The ritual is now complete, love." Issa offered her hand, and I sat up as Naya helped me off the stone table.

"I feel different. Powerful." I could feel almost the invisible strings of our bonds leading from my heart to theirs. It was a protective armor, one that made us feel nearly invincible.

"Now, we will celebrate with food, wine, and dancing!" Caro cheered, and we all laughed. We made our way back upstairs stark naked, ready to enjoy the rest of the evening.

We danced and ate to our hearts' content, celebrating the time we had together, knowing tomorrow, we would cement our powerful bonds with training and practice.

TWENTY-SIX

"Shhh. Quiet. Otherwise, you'll wake the whole goddamn coven."

I thought I must be dreaming. The voice sounded oddly familiar, but I couldn't place it. What a funny dream to feel kind of awake but not really.

"Grab her arms."

I frowned in my dream. The voice sounded menacing.

"Grab her legs."

My blissed-out sex state slowly disappeared, and I realized the voice was, in fact, not a dream. There was someone in my room. I jolted up and went to scream, but a hand clamped down on my mouth. Thrashing, I tried to free myself.

"Feisty, isn't she?" a dark voice chuckled. Slowly, the hand was replaced by a gag, all too fast for me to react.

"Fuck, I can't see a damn thing," another voice said while another pair of hands clamped down on my arms, a separate one on my legs.

A small match was lit, and I saw Saul's face hovering above mine. I tried my best to struggle, but not only were they physically restraining me, I believed there to be some magic afoot. My body felt completely locked up.

"Hello, pathetic human." His smile felt sinister.

My eyes went wide, and I scanned the room, trying to think of a way to alert the others. How had they found their way into the house without tripping the wards? I knew there were alarms set up specifically for Saul and his ignorant ass coven.

"Let her go. The magic will hold, and I'll carry her out," Saul grunted as the others nodded. Clearly, he was in charge, and whatever he said was law. He hoisted me over his shoulder, and anxiety clawed its way down my throat. I desperately shouted from my head and my heart for my body to move, but the magic was too strong.

There was no way for me to make any physical movement, no matter how desperately I commanded my muscles to do anything.

"Quiet now, so we don't wake the others," Saul whispered.

"The sleeping spell should hold, though, right?" one of his carbon copies said.

"Yes, but not for too long. Who knows how much they can resist. Their powers are unknown to us, especially if they have been moving forward with her as the fifth point. They're stronger than ever until we sever the tie," Saul grunted, and tears pricked my eyes.

Would the rest of my coven be okay? What had they used against them? Would they be able to fight it off? Would anyone know what happened to me? Would I ever be reunited with them?

Wetness stained my cheeks as Saul roughly carried me down the stairs. One of the big oafs knocked into the wall, a painting falling to the floor with a loud boom.

"Goddamnit," Saul cursed, and they all stood perfectly

still for a moment. I looked longingly at Caro, Naya, Issa, and Scar cuddled together in my bed.

They held their positions for another breath before they made their way all the way to the front door and heaved it open. There was a light shuffling somewhere in the house, and I scanned the stairs, hoping one of my beloveds had woken. Unfortunately, I saw nothing except candlelight and darkness.

They shoved the front door closed and made their way from the manor. I didn't know if it was my eyes playing tricks on me, but I swore I saw the front door open a crack and a flicker of light, but I couldn't be sure. Between the anxiety in my belly and the tears in my eyes, it was hard to tell what was and wasn't real.

"Blindfold her," Saul commended, and one of the others tied a scrap of fabric around my eyes. I tried to scurry away from his touch, but my body was still locked up. I was flopped down onto something hard and rolled a few times. I assumed we were in some sort of vehicle.

"Let's roll out, boys," Saul barked, and then we were on the move.

Tears tracked down my cheeks as I remembered how beautiful and special last night was. Would there be a way to communicate through our bond? We had no time to explore what it meant to all be connected. We were existing in that honeymoon glow, and I was so damn angry at Saul for ruining that.

Fear gripped my heart as we thudded along for what felt like eternity. The men around me were talking, but I couldn't hear them. There was a roaring in my ears that couldn't be silenced. I didn't know if it was fear, anger, or anxiety, or maybe all of them mixed it into one, but it made my body tremble and shake.

Nausea wracked its way through me. I had no idea how long it took or how much longer I would be able to take laying on this hard floor. Slowly, feeling and sensation returned to my fingertips and toes. I could wiggle some of my appendages but not all fully. My body felt sluggish and fatigued, even though my brain was wide awake and fueled by anger and fear.

Finally, we stopped, and I was pulled up again like a sack of potatoes and thrust over what I could only assume was Saul's shoulder. I wanted to scream. I tried to continue working my fingertips and toes, urging control of my wrists and ankles to return.

It was slow work, but, eventually, I got everything wiggling up to those joints until I was dumped again on a hard service, the blindfold ripped off. It took a moment for my eyes to adjust, my legs and arms still glued to my side.

"Welcome to your new home, mortal," Saul sneered while the rest of them stood around me with menacing and hungry eyes.

I was still gagged, so I just looked around at the bleakness that felt like a dark cave. My home was all warm accents and lush details, and this was barren and cold. It was dark, only a few candles lit and random bits of furniture in a large, rectangular room. Some beds were on one side, a table on another. It looked positively medieval.

Saul bent down and caressed my face. I flinched, and he chuckled as he ripped the gag away and snapped his fingers. My arms and legs were finally free while I choked and gagged on the air now filling my throat and lungs.

"The journey wasn't that rough, mortal. Don't be dramatic," Saul chided, and the others laughed obnoxiously. I didn't know what to do, so I just sat there, looking at them, my lips pressed together.

"Nothing to say, mortal?" Saul leered at me, and I scowled back at him.

"My name is Hazel," I snapped, and they all laughed again, like it was hilarious that I stood up for myself.

"Right. Well, Hazel, did you perform the bonding coven ritual?" Saul's voice adopted a serious and dark tone.

"Yes," I responded with as much confidence as I could muster.

They all cursed around me.

"Well, we will just have to sever the ties then. One step at a time, human." Saul gripped my chin hard, and I tried to pull away, but he was too strong.

"Soon, they will come for you, mortal, and we will have the home advantage. Then, you will be ours once and for all." He smiled devilishly at me.

I swallowed. Whatever had to be done to sever our bonded coven was a price I wasn't willing to pay.

TWENTY-SEVEN

Flashes of my beloveds kept coming to me. I couldn't tell if I was dreaming. It was hard to discern what was reality and what was a dream or a nightmare. Saul and his goons would spell me to be still and sleep, but time seemed to move in a funny way.

In reality, I didn't know if it had been days or hours. In my syrupy sleep haze, I saw my coven. Naya ran through the grounds, looking for me. Caro tore through the forest, desperate to find any trace left. Scarlett was calm and collected, but I could feel the rage underneath the surface of her cold stare. Issa combed through pages of books, looking for a secret to my location.

It felt like I could communicate with them somehow, give them a clue, but I had no idea how. I had no idea where Saul's hideout was, except that this area was less than desirable. I knew Saul needed to sever the connection to the coven if he wanted to have me, but I didn't know if that meant a fight to the death or something else.

I was terrified of what it would actually mean for the ones I loved. I would rather die than let Saul hurt any hair on their precious heads. Cursing, I tried to think of another way to communicate with them. The ritual had been completed. Our bonds were formed. I just needed to figure out how to access them.

Power should be able to move freely through us. I just had no time to practice. We were in a time of jubilation and celebration. The training and power could come later. We thought we had all the time in the world to explore what it meant to be together, and sadly, we were mistaken.

Saul and his minions often came and went, ignoring me like I wasn't important. I wondered what would happen if they actually tried to do something, if the bonds would prevent it. They had kept their distance thus far, so I imagined there was some magic at play here that I didn't understand.

Silently, I chastised myself for not finding out all this information sooner. No wonder it was so difficult to have a completed coven if everyone was out here snatching mortals then killing off complete covens. There was no way anyone could come out on top with this sort of anarchy.

They had just fed me, and they all were headed to bed, save for one standing guard. That detail was wholly unnecessary, considering I couldn't go anywhere or do anything with the magic crackling in the air. I felt nearly powerless. It would be silly to try and escape with so much unrecognizable power around me.

Closing my eyes, I tried to find my bonds. I pictured strings leading from my chest, connecting me to each of my loves. I focused on Caro first. I followed the string right to their chest; I could see them tearing through the woods in a ferocious cheetah form. They roared and clawed at the world around them with so much anger and pain. I wanted to hold Caro close, to tell them it was going to be okay. Pulling on the string, I tried to make a connection, but Caro was too lost in their own grief to feel the tug. I sent love down the line and tried another.

Naya was in a similar state, racing around the house, looking for any clue. In my heart, I knew she had already turned the estate over several times. Her eyes were wide and red as she screamed. I tugged on the invisible string, and she whipped her head around, looking for the source of the sensation. When she found nothing, she shook her head and stormed away. I lost the connection. My heart ached for her.

Scarlett was next. I found her standing at her bedroom window, her hands balled into fists as blood seeped from where her fingernails dug into her skin. Her features were unreadable, and I tried to reach for her heart to give her a nudge, but there was a wall up, a door of steel I couldn't get past. She had erected it to protect herself, but she didn't realize it was keeping me out. I banged against it, hoping she would feel something, but she continued to stand still and clench her jaw, more blood dripping to the ground. I sent a kiss her way and sighed.

I only had Issa left, and I hoped it would work. I didn't have a lot of faith, though, considering the others had been so filled with hurt and sorrow, they couldn't think straight.

I channeled the love I had for Issa and found the string to her heart. She was in the library, hunched over a book, a frown on her face. I pulled on the heartstring, and her eyes widened. Excited, I tried again. She rubbed her chest and closed her eyes.

I felt her consciousness meet mine through our invisible connection.

"Hazel," she breathed with a smile.

I nodded my head, afraid to say anything since I was surrounded by all of Saul's coven. The one on guard looked to be asleep, but I was afraid to chance it.

"I see you," Issa said, like she was looking around the room I was in.

Tears pricked my eyes, and I tried not to cry out.

"Hazel, we are coming for you. Don't go anywhere, I'll get the others." I watched through our connection as she gathered the others quickly and efficiently, relief on their faces. "I'm portal-ing to you. Are you ready? It will be a fight to the death, and we'll need to rely on each other's instincts and power to get this done."

I nodded again, looking around at the hulking, sleeping forms. We could take them. I knew we could. There was no other choice.

"Okay." Issa nodded, and the others stepped closer to her, grabbing her hands and breathing deep.

"Three..."

I balled my fists.

"Two..." Issa looked around.

I exhaled loudly.

"One..."

The portal opened on both ends, and it was only one breath before the whole world erupted into chaos.

Twenty-Eight

They hadn't been sleeping at all, waiting to jump into action and the fighting broke out almost immediately. An explosion erupted around us, and Scarlett screamed as she sent flames towards Saul's face.

"You bitch!" he screamed, barely dodging the heat.

A roar erupted from Caro as they charged forward in tiger form, teeth bared and claws extended. A giant brown bear met her in a sickening crunch. Someone else yelled, and I realized it was me. I could feel the claw marks in Caro's side, and it made my body ache while I sent healing from one of the others.

Naya looked at me with wide eyes and smiled, showing her teeth. I could distribute the magic around me; it felt as natural as breathing. Is this what it meant to be a connected and bound coven?

Snarling, Naya raced forward, her fangs out. She ripped into the vampire of the other coven, spraying blood everywhere. I saw Issa engaging in hand-to-hand combat with one of the other coven members. Moving like water, she struck and dodged like it was as natural as blinking.

I felt Scarlett fall and whipped my head around to see Saul

standing over her, a long sword in hand. Where the hell had he gotten that? I sent healing and opened a portal underneath her with Issa's help, sending her straight to my side in a flash. Saul looked confused and angry as he stared at where she had just been.

Scarlett relaxed into my side, the healing magic doing its work.

"What do you need, Scar?" I searched her eyes, wanting to know how I could help.

"Give me the shifting magic. I'll tear his ass apart," she spat as she stood. I nodded and sent the magic towards her from Caro, who roared happily.

Scarlett transformed into a beautiful wolf and ran towards Saul, whose mouth was wide in shock. I turned away, knowing full well this would be the end of him. He tried to throw his power at her, but it was no match for the witchcraft and shifter magic at her fingertips.

"Hazel!" Naya yelled as one of the goons tackled me, pinning me to the ground. His bloody fangs dripped with what I imagined was Naya's blood, and rage clouded my vision.

I sent Scarlett's magic to Naya, and she blasted him off with me with a gust of wind. Fire chains wrapped around him as he howled in pain, the restraints biting into his skin.

Naya reached down to help me up.

"Thank you, Naya." I gave her a quick hug and a once over, making sure there weren't any injuries I missed.

"You're doing great, princess. I'm going to finish this one off," Naya said. I swallowed, not wanting to watch. I knew what needed to be done, but that didn't mean I was used to it.

I heard Saul cry out in agony as Scarlett delivered a devastatingly fatal blow to his throat, the life draining from his eyes.

"This is for everything you have ever done to hurt any other mortal," Scarlett hissed, releasing her wolf form. "And for all the things you would have done in the future, you son of a bitch." She struck the last blow, and his lifeless form fell to the ground with a thud.

Issa had her own crony against a wall and sent an electrifying jolt through his body. I sent speed to her from Naya's own magic, and she similarly stole his life.

Naya was nearly finished with hers as well. I looked over to where Caro sat happily in her giant cat form, licking her paws covered in bear guts.

The fight had seemed so intense and so fast, but suddenly, all of them were lifeless on the ground.

"Are you okay, my love?" Issa walked over to me while the others worked on disposing the bodies.

"Yes. I was so afraid I wouldn't see you all again or that they would hurt someone. Saul said he would have to sever the bond for them to claim me, and I assumed that meant a fight to the death. I don't know what I would have done if it had been you all on the floor." My heart broke at the idea. If one of us had fallen, what would it have done to the coven? Would we have been able to pick up the pieces, or would we have fallen into despair? The thought felt heavy in my heart.

"I know, love." Issa wrapped her arms around me tightly. "We would have never let that happen. We're stronger together, and now that we are bonded and whole, we're nearly unstoppable. This fight was always going to be ours to win." She kissed my lips, and I melted into her embrace, unable to help myself.

I wanted to lose myself in all of them and leave this Saul mess behind.

"Well, it's done. The price they all needed to pay for being absolute assholes and power hungry monsters. They never knew what family or love was, just power and control." Caro spat on the ground.

"We never have to worry about them again." Naya threw

one last look around before we left, walking out of the dismal space into the open night sky. The stars shone and the moon was high. I didn't even know it was night.

Scarlett waved her hand and sent the whole place up in flames. "For Angelica." I didn't know how long we stood there, but we stared into the fire until there was nothing left but ash.

"For Angelica," we all whispered.

"Let's go home," I finally said as we linked hands. Issa sent us back to the estate, the threat of Saul no longer hanging over our heads. We were always stronger together, and we would overcome anything the world would throw our way.

TWENTY-NINE

Everyone fussed over me when we got home. Naya got me food. Scarlett bathed me. Caro gave me a massage while Issa cuddled me in bed until I fell asleep. My dreams were practically nonexistent compared to the nights before.

My brain seemed to quiet, understanding I was no longer in danger. It didn't need to reach out to my beloveds for help anymore because they were right here. I woke up alone and stretched lazily in my sheets.

Naya waltzed in carrying more food and set it down on the table next to me.

"How'd you sleep, princess?" She stroked my hair affectionately.

"Really well. I feel like a new woman." I took a small sip of water and looked at her intently.

"Are you hungry?" She offered me a piece of bread, and I shook my head.

"I'm hungry for something else." I narrowed my gaze and looked at her lovingly.

"You just got back. Are you sure you're up for it?" Naya

laughed as I nodded. Naya discarded her clothes, and I did the same, taking in her beautiful body on full display. I wanted to lick her warm skin.

"Take what you need, princess, and tell me what I can do for you." She stroked my hair as I started to kiss her belly, then her breasts. I took one nipple in my mouth and then the other as she threaded her hands through my hair. I found her clit with my fingers and stroked in time with my licks.

"Well, isn't this fun?" Scarlett said as she waltzed in without any preamble.

"Want to join?" Naya asked, and Scarlett answered by stripping down and settling behind me.

"Eat Naya's pretty little cunt, darling, and I'll eat yours from behind," Scarlett demanded, and I slid down in between Naya's legs while she lounged against the bed. My ass was in the air, and I spread my legs for Scarlett to take what she needed.

Scarlett didn't waste any time as she dove in with both her tongue and her hands. I groaned against Naya's wetness as I ate her out like I was starving, licking and devouring her essence. We groaned in unison, our orgasms building until I exploded around Scarlett. Naya was quick to follow, writhing in delicious waves of pleasure. Scarlett smacked my ass loudly and thrust her fingers inside me, wringing out another toe-curling climax as I panted against Naya's pussy.

"You're so enthusiastic when you're also getting fucked," Naya commented, pulling my mouth up to hers to taste herself.

"I came in to see how breakfast was going, but it seems like we're already satisfied." Scarlett winked as she helped me off the bed. I leaned in to kiss her, and she grabbed my ass, pulling me into her as our mouths clashed. I moved my mouth to her breasts and sucked happily while she moved her hands down to finger herself.

She came hard and fast, holding my face against her tits and sighing.

"I do love a show," Naya commented, sliding her fingers against her own clit while she watched. "You really should eat, darling. You've had a very rousing morning." Naya groaned as her eyes fluttered closed. "I just love a day started with orgasms, don't you?"

"I'm going to take a shower and get ready for the day. I love you both." I kissed Naya and then Scar before leaving them to finish their breakfasts.

I showered quickly and returned to find Caro lounging on the bed, a bulging strap on already tied around their waist. My pussy immediately started to leak down my thighs at the thought of what Caro meant to do with it.

"Hi, little one. I heard you were quite rambunctious this morning. Care for round two?" I nodded with a grin, dropping my towel as Caro stood, commanding me to bend over the bed. They teased my clit with their fingers and pulled at my already aching nipples.

"Take this like a good girl," Caro whispered.

I shivered as they started to ease the toy inside me, grabbing my hips and pumping in and out, my ass smacking against their thighs.

Issa's voice trailed in from behind me. "Oh, my love. How beautiful you look being fucked from behind." Caro pulled me up to stand with the toy still inside me.

"Be a good little one and let Issa play with you too," they whispered.

Issa stripped naked, sucking at my breasts as Caro pumped in and out of me. I felt deliciously used as Issa rubbed my clit while Caro fucked me from behind. Their mouths were everywhere at once, and I raced towards another climax, shuddering while I careened towards the edge with a grown.

"Good girl," Caro purred, pulling out of me while Issa caught me and laid me down.

"Maybe we can go for a swim, love? Since you're already a bit disheveled," Issa suggested, and we agreed to head out to the pond. Scarlett and Naya joined us, splashing and laughing as we played in the water, perfectly content with the day.

I wouldn't want to be anywhere but here, happy and safe with my beloveds. It was my fairytale dream.

EPILOGUE: ONE YEAR LATER...

We had been an official coven for a whole year, and we'd made it our mission to help others find their own covens full of love and support. We had gone from village to village, educating young ones about what it meant to be in loving, healthy relationships, and it felt like we were making a difference.

We wanted to prevent covens like Saul's from gaining traction. Covens were supposed to be about found family and support, not selfishness and deceit. We had helped bolster coven laws and hoped our work would continue to protect people in the future.

Additionally, we lobbied for and strengthened punishment surrounding coven crimes, and it seemed to be making a difference. There was a reduction in coven felonies, and we did our best to help enforce the laws whenever we could, volunteering our time and energy.

There were many completed covens popping up, full of happy and powerful beings, which was wonderful. More young beings felt empowered to make better choices than what they had been told was available to them previously.

"I like that we're helping people," I said as we left a village gathering.

"Me too. The mortal protection programs are working well, it seems." Naya smiled at the people around us. On top of our coven work, we had been trying to assist mortals since they were at the biggest risk of being taken advantage of.

"Agreed. None of it would have been possible without Hazel's help." Issa squeezed my hand.

"We do make a really great team," Scarlett mused.

"What shall we do next? Make ourselves royals?" Caro teased, and we laughed.

"No. Now, we go home and do what we do best," I said, looking around at each of them.

"And what's that, little one?" Caro hungrily looked me up and down.

"Strengthen our bond through rigorous physical training," I said innocently.

"What kind of physical training, love?" Issa looked at me with suspicion-laced eyes.

"The one that requires little clothing and me showing how much I love each and every one of you," I giggled.

"Sounds like it could take a while." Scar smirked.

Naya shrugged. "Better clear our schedules for the rest of the day, then."

"Whoever catches me gets to play first!" I took off running, the others letting me get a head start. Someone would catch me in no time, and I honestly couldn't wait.

THE END

ALSO BY MADISON NICOLE

Acknowledgments

This book would have never seen the light of day if not for the amazing people on threads who continued to tell me to publish the damn thing. Thank you for pushing me to get out of my own way.

A special thank you to Amelia who gave me the final push to get this thing out here. Your feedback was much appreciated.

Thank you to Amanda, who continues to make covers that make my heart soar.

Thank you to my editors, beta readers and every single person who made this book shine.

And thank you to my friends, family, fellow authors, readers and every single person who interacts with me on social media. You all make this possible. Thank you for supporting me every step of the way.

AUTHOR'S NOTE

This book was originally published as a chapter by chapter story online. It is the first erotica I have ever released. For some reason, it was incredibly difficult for me to hit publish on this one. Probably because this book is not my greatest literary work but it is a fucking good time. I hope you enjoyed it as much as I liked writing it!

A sneak peek into...
The Immortality
Trials

CHAPTER 1: GREER

"Another round of tequila shots, sweetheart," the man slurred.

He wasn't the first man who'd thrown out pet names while I worked my tables, and he certainly wouldn't be the last.

His half-lidded eyes raked over my body from where he was sprawled in the corner like he owned the place. The man looked human, but that didn't mean anything. Looks could be deceiving, and human or not, this large man with pale skin, a receding hairline, and an asymmetrical handlebar mustache ate me up with his eyes. It made me want to claw them out with my long black fingernails until my hands were bloody.

He was already drunk, along with the rest of his companions. All of them were impeccably dressed in dark, expensive suits, and they were throwing money around, clearly celebrating something.

"Top shelf only," another one of them bellowed.

"Absolutely, coming right up," I said with a flash of teeth through my dark red lipstick and a swish of my long wine-colored ponytail.

More alcohol means more money.

More alcohol.
More money.
I silently chanted in my head.
Ugh.

I ran over to the sleek black countertop where my bartender, Arlo, was already lining up the limes and clear liquid. He was a dragalúme, which meant his senses were heightened, and he moved with precision and grace. Not to mention, his skin was covered in iridescent scales that reflected the candles and smoky lights of the lounge.

His snow-white hair was pulled back in a low bun, so his high cheekbones and dusty white eyelashes were on full display. He wore black head to toe, with a dress shirt buttoned all the way to his throat and a pair of slacks that hit right at the ankle. The whole staff was required to wear all black at The Shadow Lounge—part of the allure, I supposed.

It was once said the dragalúme could reflect light in a way that made them nearly invisible. Light benders, according to the old texts. And apparently, they were skilled in espionage as well. At one point, they were coveted operatives by the old kingdoms, and their skills were deeply sought after, but that was long ago.

When I had asked Arlo if he could bend light after our shift one day—with a few shots making my head fuzzy and my speech bold—he snickered and said it was only a rumor. He claimed that the only thing his kind did now with their "abilities" was eavesdrop on other people's business and work more efficiently than others while looking beautiful. I knew we would be good friends after that.

Arlo gave me an apologetic smile through pale lips as he glanced over at the table of rowdy men. There were eight males in total filling up the deep green velvet couches in the corner. It was a slow night since it was a Thursday, and they were by far the loudest and rudest ones here.

A few pairs of people were milling around, but everyone else was engaging in quiet conversations on their dark velvet chairs or snuggled into alcoves, sipping leisurely on their drinks. These men had come to get plastered, and honestly, who the hell gets this hammered on a Thursday?

Usually, on Thursdays, I got let go early, but not tonight. Tonight, I would be here until the very last one of them had left, and by the looks of it, it didn't seem like they would be going anywhere any time soon.

I quickly collected the shots through a few pouty sighs.

"Greer, play nice," Arlo teased as he deftly filled other glasses with amber-colored liquid, his bone-white fingers were covered in gems that created a kaleidoscope of colors on the bar top as he worked.

Arlo knew I could take care of myself, but I'd come in with an attitude at the start of my shift, and I was having a hard time snuffing it out. Attitudes didn't equal tips, and I wanted the tips. Especially from these annoying males.

"I'm always nice," I replied with a wicked grin and a wink.

I was fine to deal with annoying and disgusting males. Most of the time. But tonight, I just wanted to go home. I wanted to sleep. And I really wanted them to leave and never hear the term sweetheart ever again.

I easily navigated through the dimly lit lounge and black glass tables. The lounge was supposed to feel dark, moody, and sensual with the mix of candles, sparkling black crystal chandeliers, and expensive cocktails. This evening, I was fitting right in with the dark and moody part.

My thigh-high black velvet boots clacked along the black marble floor as I made my way over to the table of boisterous males.

"Eight tequila shots, top shelf," I said through a smile, trying not to look like I was grimacing. One of the men, who looked to be about mid-twenties, wrapped his slightly green fingers around my wrist as I was setting down the liquor.

Ew.

"You should take a shot with us." He smirked, showing off his rows of pointed teeth. His hair was as black as his eyes and his dark navy suit almost looked like it had been painted on by how tight it wrapped around his body.

I always showed up to my shifts in a black long sleeve for this precise reason. Males liked to get handsy.

Tonight, I had chosen a leather bodysuit that circled my throat, with mesh paneling running along my ribs to my hips, fishnets, and black satin shorts. My usual array of constellation piercings studded my ears, and glittering rings accompanied my pale hands—a girl needed a little sparkle to add to the drama.

The sleeves of my bodysuit connected to my middle finger for the exact reason that I could not tolerate drunken males touching my bare skin with their greedy fingertips and hungry eyes.

Truly disgusting.

It was something that the other servers had warned me about early on, and I experienced it relatively regularly, especially since I was human. I might as well have been wearing a glaring red sign on my forehead that said, "Please try to take advantage of me because I am weak and vulnerable." Except I wasn't. I could damn well hold my own, even if society liked to pretend otherwise.

And why any male was inclined to touch anyone without their consent was beyond me. It took everything in me not to spit in his face with the darkness surrounding my mood tonight. I was practically looking for a fight at this point, but I tried to rein it in.

Rage pulsed through my veins while I grabbed the man's fingers and pried them away from my arm.

"Unfortunately, I can't drink on the job, boys," I said with a wink and a swish of my hips as I easily maneuvered out of his reach. The other men snickered, and the male hungrily followed me with his dark eyes.

"Maybe another time then, human," he said, his tongue flickering over his lips.

Go fuck yourself.

"If you're lucky," I called over my shoulder. More snickering followed.

The males stayed for three more hours, finally stumbling out around 1:00 a.m., being the last ones to go home. There was a constant stream of shots, cocktails, and bottles of champagne throughout the evening.

But at least they had tipped generously.

I don't know what you all were celebrating, but I'm glad to take your money.

Arlo and I were the last ones here as I counted the bills and rounded up the last pieces of glassware.

"Arlo, go home. I'll finish cleaning and lock up," I said.

Arlo raised one of his snow-white eyebrows and pursed his lips. "You sure?" he asked, tipping his head slightly, the small chain on his earring brushing his sharp cheekbone.

"Yeah, go home to your husband. I'll see you tomorrow," I said with a genuine smile for a genuine friend.

I didn't know how old Arlo was—could be thirty or three hundred. All specialized species lived far past the average age of a human and had the aging process to match.

"And this is why you're my favorite, dear," Arlo said, quickly finishing up the glassware and kissing me on the cheek, light as a feather. "Be careful going home. Can you please text me when you make it?" he said, stopping at the heavy black metal door.

"Of course," I said, turning my back to him and wiping

down the tables. I heard the metal door groan as Arlo cheerily said goodnight, and then it slammed shut.

I sat down on one of the plush velvet loungers and unzipped my boots and wiggled my toes. I closed my eyes and fell back on the soft cushions for a moment to relax. My feet ached, and my eyes felt heavy.

Maybe I would ask Leah to cover my shift tomorrow. I had made plenty tonight, and I was exhausted. I could curl up with a bottle of wine and see if Lux wanted to watch some terrible Netflix rom-com.

Maybe a night off would help my sour mood.

It wasn't anything in particular that was weighing heavy on me, just the fact that I was twenty-four and felt like I didn't know what the hell I was doing with my life. But, you know, it was a casual identity crisis. Not a full-blown anxiety attack, yet.

I sighed and wondered if other people felt like this. Like life was simply passing them by, and they were a bystander, not an active participant. I shook off the dramatics and told myself that I didn't need to have it all figured out. It was fine. *I* was fine.

"Are you seriously sleeping?" a deep voice sounded from the direction of the doorway.

"I'm taking a second to breathe because I had to deal with eight testosterone-charged hooligans for over four hours this evening, and I'm exhausted from my internal pity party," I said, not bothering to open my eyes. I knew that voice like I knew my own. It was my best friend Luxton, but to me, he was Lux.

He was fairly familiar with my pity parties. They had been happening quite frequently lately. Lux always listened and offered support; it was one of the many things that I absolutely adored about him. He didn't shove answers down my throat, just a steady presence of love and empathy.

I felt a shift in the lounger as he sat right next to my head. The heavy weight of him caused my head to dip. I squinted up at him.

"You didn't have to wait for me," I said.

I knew I should have texted him earlier, but those males had kept me busy most of the night. Usually, we walked home together when I worked late. It wasn't that I couldn't handle myself; it was just you didn't know what sort of things might be lurking in the shadows, and Lux worried after my pretty human head.

The Shadow Lounge was on the upper west side of Odessa, the Republic's capital city. Which was normally pretty safe, considering this was where a lot of the money was in the city. The higher up you were in the city, the more money swirled and danced around the streets. The upper west side was home to many bars, clubs, restaurants, trendy Instagram spots, and all kinds of expensive entertainment.

We lived right on the outskirts of the upper west side, so ideally, it should be fine. Except sometimes, I took shortcuts through alleys, snaking through the city to get home faster, which really didn't guarantee safety the way the well-lit streets of the city did. And one time, I had had a run in, and some male pulled a knife out on me.

I kept a switchblade on me at all times, because where I grew up you knew better than to be caught empty-handed. But he'd landed a deep gash on my forearm, and Lux had freaked out. In all fairness, as soon as that motherfucker had seen me charge him with my own weapon, he scampered away —but not before I nailed him with a slash on his chest.

But I was a human woman, a relatively easy target by society's standards, so it wasn't like Lux's worries were unfounded. *It just is what it is.*

Either way, I could take care of myself, but it was nice for him to worry. To care.

And, of course, he cared—Lux and I were roommates and best friends. The luxurious penthouse apartment we shared was courtesy of his dead parents, who, if you asked him, he had mixed emotions about them being gone. It may seem weird, but they weren't close. In fact, they had very different ideologies, the main one being that Lux's focus should have been on continuing their magic line with another shifter.

They had many heated arguments about Lux's pansexuality and his choice to not have children, and when they had died in a helicopter accident a few years ago, their entire multi-billion-dollar tech company went to their son. They had wanted to keep their magic bloodline perfect for their shifter magic, and having a son who didn't care about any of that at all was really just not in their plan for their shifter legacy.

Lux had immediately hired someone to take over and moved to be a silent partner, but he still would never need to work a day in his life if he didn't want to. He mostly worked high-end consulting jobs nowadays and worked to give money back to those who had also suffered from toxic relationships and had their sexuality used against them.

Even though his parents treated him poorly, their deaths were still hard to deal with. He had bought a whole building where rent was basically non-existent for those who needed a safe place to stay and then had sheepishly asked me to move in with him so he wouldn't be alone in the large penthouse that occupied the top floor by himself. Not only was this a truly spectacular deal for me, but I would do anything for him. We had met in college and immediately bonded over margaritas and tacos.

I had a flash of memory of the first time we went out together. He was wearing a shirt with LGBTQIA+ written across it, and I had a shirt with a pride flag. We both laughed and immediately bonded since it was literally painted on our chests what we stood for. I smiled at the memory and how we had fallen into one of those soul-deep friendships that seem to only come around once in a lifetime. We had many memories around frozen margs and tequila shots.

He never seemed to bat an eye at the fact that I didn't have a lick of magic or that I would only live to be maybe a hundred. He once told me that society and their cultural standards could go fuck themselves. I think that was really when I knew that no matter what, we would be tied together forever.

When I first moved in, Lux told me I wouldn't need to get a job if I didn't want to, and I scoffed at that. I loved living with Lux, but I sure as hell wasn't going to let him fund the rest of my life.

After graduating from college with a degree in engineering, I realized I didn't know what I was supposed to do with that. I had chosen engineering because I grew up poor. My mom told me it would be a way to save us if I could get a nice job, and at the time, I believed her. Except there was no way for my job to save her anymore.

I winced, thinking about the places I had lived in growing up. We would go from crappy motels to dirty apartments, "friends" couches, our car, to finally a steadier place that was a glorified one-bedroom townhouse. My mom had been so excited when we finally had a place of our own. It was where I learned how to wield my switchblade, hot-wire a car, and live off practically nothing.

Sometimes, it felt like a faraway dream, considering where I was now.

And some days, my life *now* felt like a dream.

My mind was a strange place sometimes.

I remember thinking that everything would be magically fixed once I graduated with a degree. As if becoming an engineer would be the saving grace of my mother's life and eliminate my own guilt and shame about the things, we did to survive that hung around my head like a cartoon rain cloud.

So now I was stuck with a degree I didn't particularly like or care for that reminded me of my dead mother.

I had worked odd jobs trying to figure out what I was supposed to do with my life until the Shadow Lounge became a full-time gig, and anything else I looked at had shit pay, even if the hours were better. And I liked the people. Arlo was the owner and the bartender, and he made me feel less alone. He made me feel seen and heard in a way so many didn't.

But I was only twenty-four years old, for gods' sake, I had plenty of time to figure my life out, right? My impending identity crisis came in waves, and right now was just a particularly low point.

In the meantime, I got to live with my best friend in a nice ass penthouse that I would probably never ever be able to afford in a million years.

So, what if my housing and lifestyle peaked in my twenties? It would be fine. *I* was fine.

"Yes, I did. We don't need you getting into knife fights regularly. I would hate to bail your ass out of jail, again," he said gently, pulling me back to the conversations as I had drifted deeper into my sour thoughts that had perturbed me this evening.

But Lux was good at that. He made me feel safe. And he did bail me out the one time I had started a bar fight in college.

I cracked a smile, remembering how some drunk idiot had tried to start a fight with Lux by taking a swing at him. Except Lux hadn't been looking, and the dumbass's face met my fist first before he could land his punch on Lux. No one messed with my best friend.

He started to untangle the ends of my ponytail with his callused dark brown hands, and I gazed lovingly up at him. Lux was breathtakingly handsome. His thick black hair was in braids today, reaching down his back and tied loosely with a piece of black fabric. His gold eyes were bright and framed with dark, thick lashes. His bone structure made everyone swoon as his sculpted cheekbones matched his perfectly sculpted cupid's bow and studded nose.

He was broad and muscular, with tattoos swirling around most of his six-two dark brown body. He wore the tattoos like an accessory, changing them some days or keeping some for years. The advantage of being a shapeshifter was that he could manipulate any part of his body on a whim. But he kept this image pretty consistently as his own.

However, shifters long ago were punished for shifting into other's identities. It was the Republic's way of keeping them in check. Everyone was required to have a way to be easily IDed that matched who they were in the Republic's system.

So, this was the version of Lux I had always known. Bright eyes, dark skin, handsome as sin. Everyone always tried to put us together, but in reality, there was absolutely zero romantic interest from either party. It was easy for them to assume I was his arm candy since not very many of the wealthy and powerful toted around humans as more than playthings.

But our love was one of family, not romance or lust.

"Can you snap your fingers and have this place cleaned up and us on the couch at home?" I whined, shutting my eyes and turning to bury my face into his thigh.

He laughed darkly and replied, "I'm not a witch or a tele-porter, but maybe we should find some and befriend them to help you next time."

Groaning, I sat up and rolled through my neck. I could do this. Taking a deep breath, I looked at Lux and said, "Okay, fifteen minutes. Feel free to time me."

I winked before I vaulted up and started racing around the room without my boots, quickly trying to clean up the mess that all our patrons had made this evening.

"Done," I shouted, panting slightly. Sweat dripped down

my brow, and I rapidly wiped it away with the back of my sleeve.

Lux gave me an amused smile and uncrossed his jean-clad legs, smoothed out his white shirt, adjusted the lapels on his camel-colored coat, and stood up.

"Fourteen minutes and fifty-eight seconds. Not the best, but Arlo will love you all the same." He snickered. "Let's go."

I swiftly zipped up my boots and grabbed my purse, then shrugged on my red faux fur coat and shut off the lights. I walked through the heavy metal door and locked it tight.

"Let's go home," I said. I looped my arm through his and laid my head on his shoulder as we walked through the quiet city streets bathed in moonlight.